TOO GOOD TO BE TRUE

Suzanne rose from the couch and wound her arms about Mr. Collins's neck. She could feel his muscles tensing as she pressed up against him.

"Suzanne, stop it," Mr. Collins warned.

She parted her lips and tilted her head back, willing him to embrace her. He was so close. His heart was beating much too quickly. . . .

Trembling with the effort, Mr. Collins pulled free from her. "Get your things," he ordered. "I'll wait for you in the car."

She stared at him for a long, incredulous moment. How *dare* he reject her?

Her eyes narrowed to razor-thin slits. "You wanted to kiss me. I know you did."

Mr. Collins shook his head. "Believe me, I'm doing you a favor."

But Suzanne scarcely heard what he was saying. Rage was boiling inside her. Oh, he'd pay for this. She'd make him pay.

"*You're* the one who's going to be sorry, Roger Collins!" she hissed.

Bantam Books in the Sweet Valley High Series
Ask your bookseller for the books you have missed

SWEET VALLEY HIGH

TOO GOOD TO BE TRUE

Written by
Kate William

Created by
FRANCINE PASCAL

BANTAM BOOKS
TORONTO • NEW YORK • LONDON • SYDNEY • AUCKLAND

RL 5, IL age 12 and up

TOO GOOD TO BE TRUE
A Bantam Book / August 1984

Sweet Valley High is a trademark of Francine Pascal

Conceived by Francine Pascal

Produced by Cloverdale Press Inc.,
133 Fifth Avenue, New York, N.Y. 10003

Cover art by James Mathewuse

ISBN 0-553-24252-0

Published simultaneously in the United States and Canada

PRINTED IN THE UNITED STATES OF AMERICA

O   0 9 8 7 6 5 4 3 2

To Taryn Rebecca Adler

edy act," suggested the twins' nineteen-year-old brother, Steven, who was home from college for the weekend. His dark eyes twinkled. "Like the Smothers Brothers."

"Very funny." Jessica sniffed. "Anyway, if I don't get to go to New York, I'll be too broken-hearted to go to college. I'll probably just sit home and waste away to nothing." She crammed a huge forkful of mashed potatoes into her mouth.

Elizabeth took a more sensible approach. "You could flip a coin," she suggested to her father. "You know, like you used to do when we were little and we both wanted something there was only one of. You remember the time you won that doll at the fair and Jessica—"

"Yeah, Dad gave it to me and then felt so sorry for you he went out and bought you an ever better one," Jessica finished, frowning at the memory.

But this wasn't some dumb doll, Jessica thought. This was a trip to the most exciting city in the world. She had to go—somehow. If ping a coin didn't win her the opportunity, find another way. And when it came to ng what she wanted, few things ever stood n Jessica's path.

Her mind drifted. She imagined herself whirling breathlessly beneath the flashing lights of some impossibly chic Manhattan disco. *Suddenly a hand touches her arm. She turns. "Pardon me,"* Mick Jagger *says, "I believe this next dance is mine."*

Or she would be strolling through the glittering aisles of Tiffany's, and the owner would rush up to her, holding out a priceless emerald necklace. *"It's made for you, my dear,"* he says. *"Look how the jewels match your eyes." He waves aside her protests that she can't afford such an expensive necklace. "No, you must consider it a gift. It's payment enough for me just to see you wearing it."*

She might even be discovered by one of the top modeling agencies. She could become the next Cheryl Tiegs. Within a few weeks, her face would be on the cover of *Cosmopolitan*. Jessica felt a tingle of electric excitement trace its way up her spine. She *had* to go—she simply *had* to.

"Yeah, Dad, why don't you flip a coin," Steven was saying. "A nice clean kill so we don't have to listen to these two squabbling about it for the next century."

"Why, Steve, I don't know what you could possibly mean," Jessica purred. "Liz and I almost never argue. No one could ask for a sweeter, more *generous* sister."

"Forget it, Jess," Elizabeth cut in. "I'm not *that* generous, in case you're getting any ideas. I still think the best solution is for Dad to flip a coin. At least that way no one can say it wasn't fair."

"I second the motion," Mrs. Wakefield put in. "Ned, you'd better flip a coin before this conversation goes any further."

With her trim, youthful good looks, Alice Wakefield could almost have passed for the twins' older sister. Elizabeth and Jessica had inherited their sunshine-blond hair and blue-green eyes from her. The two girls looked exactly alike—each even had a dimple in her left cheek when she smiled. But that was where the similarity ended. While Elizabeth was fairness personified, Jessica prided herself on being clever and devious. Steven was more like Elizabeth, although he looked like a carbon copy of their tall, dark-haired, athletic father.

Mr. Wakefield dug into his pocket for a quarter. "Sounds like a good idea," he said. "Besides, I don't hear anyone coming up with a better one."

Their father was so infuriatingly fair, Jessica thought. She supposed it must come from being a lawyer. Why couldn't he be unfair for a change? Unfair to Elizabeth, that is.

"We could take turns," Jessica said hopefully. "I'll go this time, and Liz can go next."

Elizabeth reached over and gave her sister a playful swat.

Mr. Wakefield balanced the quarter on the back of his thumb. "Anyone for heads?"

"Tails," Jessica spoke out. Taking the different route had always been her trademark.

"Guess that leaves me with heads," Elizabeth said. The truth was, she didn't feel nearly so anxious as Jessica obviously did.

Jessica covered her eyes. "Oh, God, the suspense is killing me! I can't watch!"

It *had* to be tails. Jessica imagined how jealous her friends would be when she told them. The Devlins were rich. They probably lived in a penthouse on Park Avenue. She would eat at the fanciest restaurants, drive around in limousines, meet fabulously wealthy men. . . .

"Heads," Mr. Wakefield announced.

Jessica's eyes flew open. *It couldn't be!* Maybe she hadn't heard right. But one look at her sister's happy face and she knew it was true. Jessica burst into tears.

Elizabeth placed a compassionate arm about her sister's quivering shoulders. "I'm sorry, Jess. Really I am. I wish there were some way we could both go. But, listen, I'm sure there'll be other chances."

"Never!" Jessica sobbed. "I'll probably never set foot out of this dumb town for the next hundred and thirty-seven years!"

"Come on, Jess, you're exaggerating."

But Elizabeth's attempt to comfort her twin was greeted only by a fresh outburst of wailing. Jessica wasn't about to be consoled.

"You can wear my new culottes while I'm gone if you like," Elizabeth offered as she was getting ready for bed. "They look better on you anyway."

Jessica, who was lying face down on Elizabeth's bed, unburied a blotchy, mournful face. "Bribery will get you nowhere."

Elizabeth sighed. "Look, it's not as though I cheated or anything. It could just as easily have been you."

"The point is," Jessica said, sniffing, "it *wasn't* me."

"OK, but I was only trying to make you feel better."

"Somehow a pair of culottes doesn't exactly compare with a trip to New York."

"Oh, come on, it won't be so bad here. What about the class picnic? And you won't have to miss Lila's big birthday bash at the country club, either. At least you won't be sitting around with nothing to do."

As for herself, Elizabeth wasn't sorry to be missing Lila Fowler's party. The Fowlers, especially Lila, were snobs in her opinion, though for once they'd done the fair thing and invited the whole junior class instead of just a popular few. She was sorry that she wouldn't be able to go to the picnic, though. She *had* been looking forward to it. In fact, she was supposed to write an article about it for *The Oracle*, Sweet Valley High's newspaper. Elizabeth was one of the school's best journalists, as well as the author of *The Oracle*'s "Eyes and Ears" gossip column. Now someone else would have to take over the picnic assignment. She frowned. That was only one of the things she'd be missing while she was in New York.

Jessica could see that Elizabeth was having second thoughts, and she felt her hopes rise. Maybe there was still a way. . . .

"You're right, Liz," she said. "I guess I am being pretty babyish about all this. I really am looking forward to Lila's party." Jessica's aquamarine eyes sparkled with devilish intent. "Too bad *you'll* have to miss it, though. Poor Todd—I guess he'll end up going by himself."

Elizabeth thought about how much she'd miss her boyfriend. Two weeks away from him would seem like forever. "I hope he won't be too lonely," she said, biting her lip.

"Oh, I'm sure he won't be for long," Jessica reassured her worried sister. "Todd's too good-looking for that."

Elizabeth frowned. "What's that supposed to mean?"

"Oh, you probably have nothing to worry about. It's just that—" she hesitated—"well, I really shouldn't be telling you this, since it's supposed to be a secret and all . . ."

"What?" Elizabeth practically shrieked.

"Well, the thing is Lila has always had this sort of, uh, crush on Todd."

"Lila? Are you sure?"

"Positive. She told me so herself. She said that if you were ever out of the picture—well, she just didn't know how she could control herself around Todd. Oh, but I'm sure nothing would come of it—even though Lila *is* a knockout. Todd loves *you*."

Lila was pretty, all right, Elizabeth thought. Pretty enough to tempt even the most faithful of boyfriends. She was rich, too. Though, of course, Todd wouldn't . . . would he?

"I'm not worried," Elizabeth lied.

"No reason to be. Like I said, I'm sure nothing will come of it." Jessica got up to examine her reflection in the mirror. "It's just that you *know* how determined Lila can be when she wants something."

"Sounds like somebody else I know," Elizabeth observed dryly.

Jessica pretended not to hear. "She's a horri-

9

ble flirt. She's always bragging that she hasn't come across any boy yet who's been able to resist her."

"No one could ever accuse Lila of being humble, that's for sure."

Jessica picked up Elizabeth's brush and ran it through her hair, pretending to be nonchalant. "Besides, even if she *did* get somewhere with Todd, I'm sure it wouldn't last. He's not really her type."

"Gee, Jess, you really know how to put a person at ease," Elizabeth remarked sarcastically. "What do you expect me to do about it anyway?"

"You could always stick around to keep Lila from getting any ideas," Jessica suggested sweetly.

"I think I'm beginning to get the picture."

Jessica whirled to face her sister. "Don't you see, Liz? You'd be doing yourself a big favor by letting me go to New York in your place."

"I don't believe this!"

"OK, but if you think I'm making up what Lila said, you can ask Cara. She was there, too."

Elizabeth sank down on the bed and groaned. "Why do I have the feeling I'm being talked out of going on this trip?"

Jessica sprinted across the room to throw her arms around her sister. "Oh, Liz, I'll never forget this! You're the dearest, sweetest, most ador-able sister in the whole universe!"

"Wait a minute, I never said—"

But Jessica wasn't listening. She was already streaking downstairs, singing out, "Guess what, everybody? Liz offered to let me go to New York in her place. Isn't that the most generous thing you ever heard?"

Two

"I still can't believe it!" Jessica cried. "Oh, Liz, it's like a dream come true. I'm so excited I could faint!"

"Don't you dare faint on me now," Elizabeth warned. "I couldn't carry one single thing more."

Buried under the mound of carry-on luggage she was holding for Jessica, Elizabeth managed a breathless little laugh. Their parents and Steven, who was home from college on mid-semester break, had gone off to see about Suzanne's plane, which would be arriving soon after Jessica's took off, if all went according to schedule. Jessica took one last look at her makeup in a pocket-size mirror.

Satisfied, she slipped the mirror back into her purse and sighed. "I really *do* wish you were coming, Liz. Honestly, it's not going to be the same without you." For a change, she was being sincere.

"Thanks, Jess, but actually it's better this way. You know I've never been all that crazy about big-city life. Besides, we don't even know the Devlins. I'd feel funny staying with perfect strangers."

A tiny frown creased Jessica's forehead. "Well, *I* happen to adore big cities," she stated defensively. "If you want to be stuck in this crummy little cowpatch for the rest of your life, it's OK by me, but I intend to live it up while I'm still young enough to enjoy it. Big Apple, here I come!"

Elizabeth couldn't resist a smile at her sister's enthusiasm. "I can see you're ready for New York. The question is, is New York ready for *you*? Just don't get too carried away, OK?"

"Who, me?" Jessica cast her sister a look of utter innocence. "When was the last time I got too carried away?"

"When was the last time you *didn't*?"

Jessica tried hard to hold her frown, but it dissolved in a sputter of laughter. "How come if we're identical twins you don't have *my* sense of adventure?"

"Don't worry," Elizabeth said. "I plan to have a few adventures of my own while you're away. You may have New York, but remember, *I* have Todd."

Jessica's eyes took on a faraway, dreamy look. "I hear there are tons of exciting men in New York. Lila was there last summer, and she said they were *everywhere*."

"Just watch out," Elizabeth said, deadpan. "One of them might try to snatch your purse."

Jessica socked her sister's arm in mock outrage. "You're just jealous because you're not going."

Elizabeth thought for a moment before answering. "You know something? I'm really not. Otherwise, I never would have let you wangle me into trading places. I may be nice, but not *that* nice. If I'd really wanted to go, nothing could have made me change my mind."

It was the truth. After thinking it over this past week, Elizabeth decided she was satisfied with the arrangement. As far as vacation went, her sense of adventure and fun was far different from Jessica's. She would have preferred to go mountain climbing in the Sierras or rafting down the Colorado River. Then there was the *Oracle* article. Besides, Lila or no Lila, she really would have missed Todd. They'd made plans to spend a lot of time together over the school break, and Elizabeth would have hated to miss that. No, it was better this way. Let Jessica have the glamour and glitter of New York. Knowing Jessica, she would make the most of it in a way few people could match.

"All set!" Mr. Wakefield called out as he made his way toward the twins across the crowded terminal.

Mrs. Wakefield filled them in on the details. "Suzanne's plane is due in half an hour. It's too bad you won't get to meet her, Jess, but your plane is going to be boarding any minute. We'd better get down to the gate if you don't want to miss it."

"Wouldn't that be awful if you did miss your plane?" Elizabeth said as they lined up to have the luggage x-rayed.

Steven laughed. "Yeah, then we'd be stuck with Jess for another two whole weeks!"

"Thanks a lot, you guys." Jessica said, pretending to look hurt. "I didn't expect you to be heartbroken that I was leaving, but I thought you might at least miss me just a teensy bit."

"Are you kidding?" Steven slung an affectionate arm about Jessica's shoulders. "What are we going to do without you around to stir things up? Life could get pretty dull."

Jessica let that one pass without comment. She was distracted when her turn came to pass through the metal detector. A loud buzzing alarm

15

sounded, causing Jessica to flush with embarrassment. A guard motioned her to the side.

Elizabeth giggled. "Maybe he thinks you're carrying a weapon. I can just see the headlines: 'Teenager Hijacks Plane To Disneyland.' "

"That's *not* funny," Jessica said as she removed the heavy silver bracelet that had caused the problem.

A moment later, they were sailing into the boarding area. Jessica threw her arms around each of them in turn. She said her goodbyes amid tears and extravagant promises to write.

"It's only for two weeks, Jess," Elizabeth reminded her following her twin's crushing embrace. "Honestly, anyone would think you were going to be gone for at least a year."

Jessica threw up her hands. "Who knows? Maybe I'll love it so much, I'll decide never to come back!"

"Is that a threat or a promise?" Steven teased.

"Say hi to King Kong for me!" Elizabeth called in final farewell as Jessica disappeared onto the plane.

The Wakefields peered expectantly through the huge window of the terminal as Suzanne Devlin's plane taxied into the gate.

"Tom tells me she's pretty involved with

sports," Mr. Wakefield said. "Tennis, jogging, horseback riding, swimming—you name it."

"Great," Elizabeth said. "Maybe we can do a little water-skiing, too, while she's here."

"Watch out," said Steven. "She might be having such a good time she'll want to stick around. Can you imagine Jessica having to share her room? Poor Jess."

Elizabeth giggled. "Poor Suzanne, you mean. We'd have to invent a new sport just for wading through that junkpile Jess calls a room. Suzanne's probably used to better accommodations, though."

"I'll bet she's used to living away from home," Mrs. Wakefield mused. "Ned, didn't you say she's gone to boarding schools most of her life?" She sighed. "I suppose there's nothing wrong with it, but I don't see how I ever could have sent you kids away like that. Maybe I'm just old-fashioned, but I think children belong at home until they're ready for college."

Steven laughed. "Look at me—I'm going to college and you're *still* stuck with feeding me practically every weekend. Not to mention my dirty laundry."

Their mother chuckled. "Now *that* I wouldn't miss."

"I'll bet she's really sophisticated." Elizabeth

sighed. "I've never met anyone who's gone to boarding schools in Europe. I thought that was something they only did in books. She'll probably make the rest of us look like hopeless idiots."

"Speak for yourself," Steven growled, jostling her affectionately with his elbow.

The passengers were beginning to trickle out into the terminal. Elizabeth strained to see past a couple with three pudgy children and a mountain of carry-on luggage. Would Suzanne recognize them from the picture Mom had sent?

Abruptly Elizabeth drew in her breath. Walking toward them was the most beautiful girl she'd ever seen. Suzanne? No, she couldn't be! This girl had to be a professional model—or an actress. She was tall and willowy, with black hair that tumbled in glossy waves past her shoulders. Her back was bare in a chic sun dress she'd obviously worn in anticipation of the good weather. Her features couldn't have been more perfect if they'd been sculpted by Michelangelo. Elizabeth was most struck by her enormous, dark-fringed, violet-blue eyes, which were now searching the crowd outside the gate. Suddenly she spotted the Wakefields and swooped down on them with a squeal of recognition.

"Elizabeth!" she cried. "I'd know you anywhere, though that picture your parents sent didn't do you justice. You're even prettier than I expected."

Elizabeth could only stammer some unintelligible reply.

Mrs. Wakefield enveloped their guest in a warm embrace. "Welcome to Sweet Valley, Suzanne! We're so delighted to have you here."

Suzanne broke into a dazzlingly brilliant white smile. "Oh, I've wanted to visit for ages." She turned to Ned Wakefield. "Dad talks about you all the time, Mr. Wakefield. And when he had this idea for me to come out and visit"—she gave a silvery little laugh—"well, wild horses couldn't have kept me away."

She spoke with an enchanting accent that was vaguely British-sounding. Probably from living in Europe, Elizabeth thought, awestruck by Suzanne's sophistication. She didn't sound stuck-up, though, the way Jessica had when she was playing the lead in *My Fair Lady* the year before and had gone around school talking in an English accent for weeks. Suzanne was obviously the genuine article.

"Tom did say you were into horseback riding, now that you mention it." Mr. Wakefield laughed as he reached for the tote bag Suzanne was carrying. They headed toward the baggage pickup area. "I just hope you won't find Sweet Valley dull compared to the lights of the city."

"Oh, Dad," Elizabeth scolded playfully. Life in Sweet Valley, as far as she was concerned, was far from dull. But even if it was, Suzanne's arrival was sure to liven things up in a hurry.

Suzanne hooked her arm through Elizabeth's. "I just know I'm going to love it."

Any shadow of doubt Elizabeth might have had about letting Jessica take her place in New York was gone. Now that she'd met Suzanne, the prospects for having fun appeared endless. Suzanne seemed as friendly and enthusiastic as she was glamorous.

The ride from the airport to the Wakefields' split-level ranch house was peppered with little cries of delight from Suzanne as she gazed out the window, exclaiming over how green and lush everything was and what a "perfectly adorable" town Sweet Valley was. She asked Elizabeth a lot of questions, about where the kids from Sweet Valley High hung out during vacations and where the best places to shop were. Elizabeth promised to show her everything, starting with the junior class picnic the next day.

"It's a tradition every spring break. We all go up to the lake to swim, and then afterward there's a big barbecue," she explained. "This way you'll get to meet everyone at once. I hope you remembered to bring a bathing suit."

She laughed. "Are you kidding? The minute I heard you had a pool. . . . I just hope I don't stand out. Everyone around here is so tan. I'll look white as a sheet!"

"Don't worry," Elizabeth assured her. "It doesn't take long to get brown in this kind of weather. Besides, you're bound to stand out no matter what. In fact, you may need a body-guard after the guys get a look at you."

Suzanne smiled. "Oh, Elizabeth, you're too much."

"Please call me Liz."

"OK, Liz. And you can call me Suzy. That's what my friends back home call me. Although Pete, my boyfriend, just calls me Devlin. Do you have a steady boyfriend?"

Elizabeth flushed. It was the reaction she generally had when the subject of Todd came up. She was always certain that people could look right through her and see what was in her heart. Her deepest feelings about Todd weren't ones she felt comfortable sharing, even with her closest friends.

"You'll meet him at the picnic," she replied.

"I can hardly wait!"

Suzanne tried drawing Steven into the conversation, too, but though it was obvious he was just as dazzled by Suzanne as the rest of them, he had his mind elsewhere. As they passed through the neighborhood where his girlfriend Tricia Martin lived, he stared out the window, a sad expression on his face. Elizabeth knew he was thinking about Tricia, worrying about their relationship. They'd always been so devoted to one another, but lately, Steven had complained, Tricia seemed to be drawing away from him. It almost seemed as if she were avoiding him.

It was true she was having trouble at home. Her father had been arrested recently for drunk driving after he hit a pedestrian, and though he was out on bail now it was easy to see why Tricia would be upset. Elizabeth sometimes ran into her at school, where Tricia was a senior, and her worries were evident from the strained look on her face these days. But wouldn't she want Steven around to help comfort her? Why was she acting so distant? It didn't make sense. Whatever the problem, Steven was so in love with Tricia, the prospect of losing her sent him into a panic.

As soon as they got home, Steven immediately went to phone Tricia. Elizabeth could hear his muffled voice on the downstairs phone as she walked upstairs to help Suzanne unpack in Jessica's room.

"Trish, is that you? . . . You sound funny. . . . Is this a bad time to talk? . . . Do you want me to call back? . . . OK. . . . No, it's all right, I don't mind. . . . Hey, I love you. Trish? Did you hear me?"

Elizabeth felt so sorry for Steven. Things sounded worse than ever between Tricia and him. She heard a choked cry of frustration as he hung up the phone, and she winced in sympathy.

Elizabeth made herself turn her attention back to Suzanne. It wouldn't be fair to involve Suzanne in Steven's problems during her first hour there.

When they'd finished unpacking, the girls slipped into their bathing suits to go for a dip in the pool. They were both hot and sweaty after the drive from the airport. Suzanne, despite her embarrassment over being so pale, looked absolutely stunning in her striped bikini. She was flawlessly proportioned, with legs that seemed to go on forever, and not an ounce of fat anywhere. Suddenly Elizabeth felt self-conscious about her own lovely size-six figure.

It wasn't all decoration with Suzanne either. She could really swim. After a dozen or so laps, she was barely winded. Elizabeth collapsed onto the deck, gasping for breath.

"Wow, you're really in good shape," Elizabeth said breathlessly. "I'll bet even your boyfriend has a hard time keeping up with you."

Suzanne gave a laugh, tossing her wet hair so that it sparkled in the sunlight as it released a spray of droplets. "Oh, don't worry about Pete. He manages to follow me just about everywhere. I hate to say this, because I don't want to seem stuck-up, but sometimes I think maybe he's *too* much in love with me."

To Elizabeth it sounded strange. She could never think Todd was too much in love with her, but then Suzanne probably had a million guys chasing after her. Maybe it was hard getting attached to just one when you had so many to choose from. Like trying to choose what flavor of ice cream to have at Baskin-Robbins.

"Aren't you in love with him?" Elizabeth asked.

Suzanne shrugged. "Oh, sure. I guess I just don't like the idea of being tied down, that's all. My parents practically have me married off to Pete."

"But you're only sixteen!"

"They sent me away to school when I was nine. It's the same thing. They can't wait to get rid of me."

Suzanne didn't appear to be too unhappy about it, but Elizabeth was stunned. How could anyone's parents be so callous? She wondered if her father knew about this side of the Devlins. He had always spoken so highly of Mr. Devlin in the past. Poor Suzanne! And poor Jessica! What would it be like to spend two weeks with people like that?

Nevertheless, the life Suzanne went on to describe to Elizabeth sounded anything but boring. Zipping around New York City in Pete's Ferrari. Moonlight sails on his father's yacht. Debutante balls. Skiing in Aspen. Even if Elizabeth wouldn't have wanted to trade places with her, she couldn't help thinking it all seemed like a fairy tale.

That night, they ate dinner out on the patio— barbecued spareribs, potato salad, and a lemon chiffon pie Elizabeth had made in their guest's honor. Suzanne kept praising the meal, especially the pie, which had been made from lemons that grew in the Wakefields' backyard. Afterward she declared she'd never been so stuffed in her whole life. Then she insisted on doing the dishes, even though Mrs. Wakefield told her she should rest after her long trip. Suzanne wouldn't hear of it, though. Waving aside everyone's protests, she bustled about the kitchen. Within minutes, it was spotless.

"Better watch out," Elizabeth warned Suzanne as they were on their way to bed later that evening. "If you keep up that kind of thing, we may never want you to leave."

Suzanne giggled. "Is that a threat or a promise?"

"You'd know which if you had to share a room with Jessica," Elizabeth said laughingly.

"I wouldn't mind. I've always wanted a sister. Twin sisters would be even better. Double the fun."

"It must be hard, being an only child."

Suzanne's expression darkened momentarily, but then she shrugged and gave Elizabeth one of her sparkly smiles. "Well, I can't have everything. Besides, what's the point in getting depressed over something I can't change? I've always believed in looking on the positive side of things. I guess I'm just naturally optimistic."

"I know what you mean," Elizabeth said. "Once in a while I wake up in the morning and don't feel like getting out of bed. Then I think of all the fun things I'd be missing if I didn't." She glanced at her watch. "Speaking of bed, we should probably get some sleep. I'm supposed to be at the picnic early to help with the food. You don't mind, do you?"

"Mind? I love helping! And I can't wait to meet all your friends. Especially Todd—he sounds divine." Impulsively, she hugged Elizabeth. "Oh, Liz, I just know this is going to be the best vacation I've ever had!"

Elizabeth hugged her back. "I certainly hope so."

"Oh, it will be." Suzanne's grin lit up the room. "I *never* have boring vacations."

Three

"Pass me the mustard . . . pass me the pickles
. . . but *pleeease* don't pass me by," Winston
Egbert crooned.

On bent knee he serenaded Suzanne, strum-
ming energetically on his guitar while he impro-
vised in a loud, off-key voice. His spiky black
hair stood on end from a recent dive into the
lake, and his ears were fire-engine red from
sunburn, making him look even more comical
than usual. As he sang, his Adam's apple bobbed
up and down his scrawny throat.

Suzanne laughed, tossing her silky black hair
over one lightly toasted shoulder as she sat on a
picnic table bench. "You should be in the Grand

Ol' Opry, Winston,'' she teased. ''Why are you wasting your talents on me?''

Ever the clown, he rolled his eyes and placed his hand over his heart. ''Can't you see I'm in love?''

Someone snickered. ''I think Winston's lost his marbles.''

''I didn't know he had any left to lose,'' joked blond, muscular Tom McKay, popping open a can of soda.

Handsome Bruce Patman—who, along with a few other seniors had been invited to the picnic—turned his reflector sunglasses in Suzanne's direction. ''I don't see what's so crazy about a guy falling for a foxy lady like Suzanne here.''

Several people exchanged surprised looks. Super-popular, super-cool Bruce usually waited for the girls to beat a path to his door rather than the other way around. Clearly, he, too, had joined the ranks of the admirers of the fabulous Suzanne Devlin.

''It's a good thing Jessica is three thousand miles away,'' murmured Enid Rollins, Elizabeth's best friend. They were sitting together at a picnic table near the one where Suzanne was sitting. ''If she saw all the attention Suzanne's been getting, she'd be the only one here who was green instead of tan.''

Enid was attracting a few stares of her own in

her new candy-striped bathing suit, Elizabeth had noticed. Though she wasn't stunning like Suzanne, Enid, with her shiny, shoulder-length brown hair and enormous green eyes, had a prettiness that was all her own.

Elizabeth smiled. "What Jessica doesn't know won't hurt her."

"As long as George doesn't become a member of the Suzanne Devlin Fan Club, she can stay forever as far as I'm concerned," Enid said, George being her steady boyfriend. A freshman at Sweet Valley College, he was her guest at the picnic that day.

"I know what you mean. I was a little worried about Todd at first, too. But I suppose you can't blame the guys for looking. Who wouldn't? She's so incredibly beautiful."

Despite all the attention she was getting, Suzanne didn't appear to be letting it go to her head. She was as friendly to the girls as to the boys, talking and kidding around as if she'd known everyone for most of her life. And when it came time to help with the food, she was the first one to pitch in.

"She's almost too good to be true," Enid said, spreading a thin layer of catsup over her hamburger bun. "Gosh, I wonder what it would be like to be so gorgeous and sophisticated."

"*I'll* tell you if you're really interested," Cara

Walker drawled. No conversation was too sacred for eavesdropping as far as Cara was concerned.

She reached across the picnic table for the salt shaker, holding it up to her lips as if it were a microphone.

"It's not easy being a ten, folks. Do you know what it's like having your phone ring day and night? Can you imagine being wakened up at all hours by guys serenading you outside your window? I'm telling you, it's a tough life."

"Dream on, Cara," snickered Lila, who was sitting next to her. Dark-eyed, olive-skinned Cara Walker was certainly attractive, but nowhere near Suzanne's league.

Elizabeth and Enid nearly choked on their hamburgers from laughing so hard. Even Todd joined in, waggling a pickle spear under his nose à la Groucho Marx as he pretended to ogle Cara.

It was the most fun Elizabeth could ever remember having at a class picnic. The weather was just right, the lake was a perfect temperature, and everybody seemed to be in a good mood. Even Mr. Collins, who had agreed to act as chaperon and unofficial lifeguard, seemed to be having a good time.

Roger Collins was faculty adviser to *The Oracle*, as well as one of the most popular teachers at

Sweet Valley High. And it was simple to see why. In addition to his good looks and easygoing manner, he was always there for the students when they needed someone to talk to, when they were having problems in school or at home.

Right then, Mr. Collins was officiating at the barbecue grill, passing out sizzling hamburgers along with samples of his dry wit. Elizabeth noticed Suzanne following his movements with her eyes. Well, why not? Roger Collins was without a doubt the best-looking teacher at Sweet Valley High. With his windblown, strawberry-blond hair and crinkly blue eyes, he reminded Elizabeth a little of Robert Redford.

After everyone had finished eating, some of the kids set up a net and got a volleyball game going. An hour later, they were ready for a nice cool swim. Suzanne was the first to hit the water, stroking her way toward the far end of the lake. Enid and George got into a water fight that soon escalated into an all-out war. No one within firing range was safe. Todd commented jokingly to Elizabeth that it was beginning to look more like Marine World than a picnic.

Suddenly Elizabeth noticed a tiny figure out in the middle of the lake who appeared to be floundering.

"Mr. Collins!" she yelled. "I think Suzanne's in trouble!"

Mr. Collins took one look, and instantly he was in the water, thrashing his way toward her with powerful strokes. Elizabeth remembered him telling her once that he'd been a lifeguard in college. She watched with growing relief as he began maneuvering Suzanne toward shore, one arm looped about her chest. The crowd broke into cheers when he had finally scooped her out of the water and carried her up the beach. A very drenched-looking Suzanne clung to him, sobbing.

"I—I don't know what happened," she choked. "I must have gone too far. My legs just g-gave out on me." Mr. Collins tried to put her down, but she wrapped her arms about his neck even more tightly, burying her face against his muscular chest. "Oh, Mr. Collins, if it hadn't been for you, I might have drowned!"

"Are you all right now?" he asked.

"Well . . . sort of. I know this will probably sound silly, but I'd feel so much better if you could just sit with me for a few more minutes. I—I still feel kind of wobbly."

Mr. Collins looked uncomfortable. "If you're not feeling well, maybe someone should take you home."

"Oh, no, please, I wouldn't want to put anyone out. Besides, I'm feeling much better now. You can put me down. I promise I won't collapse." She offered a shaky smile.

Mr. Collins didn't argue.

As it turned out, Suzanne had no shortage of strong shoulders to lean on. As soon as Mr. Collins left, she was surrounded by more than a dozen concerned males, eager to offer their support and sympathy. Aaron Dallas, co-captain of the soccer team, tenderly wrapped his towel around her, while Tom McKay held her hand until she stopped shivering. In an effort to cheer her up, Winston strummed another one of his made-up melodies about a fair lady lost at sea. Even Bruce Patman got in on the action by bringing her a paper cupful of iced tea.

Elizabeth was left with a vague feeling of confusion. Something was wrong, and she tried hard to put her finger on what was bothering her. Then she thought about the other day when she and Suzanne had swum laps in the pool. Suzanne was such a strong swimmer. How had she come so near to drowning?

"You look a little shaky yourself," Todd said, slipping an arm about Elizabeth's waist. "That was a close call."

Elizabeth swiveled around to face him, momentarily forgetting her consternation over Suzanne. Todd smiled down at her, his brown eyes filled with tenderness. His dark hair curled in damp ringlets, and beads of moisture glistened on his broad, sun-burnished chest.

"I'm just glad she's OK," Elizabeth said. "If it hadn't been for Mr. Collins . . ."

"Are you kidding? Another few seconds and she would've had more rescuers than she knew what to do with."

"It's funny how Mr. Collins was acting," Elizabeth observed thoughtfully. "Almost like he couldn't wait to get away afterward."

"Maybe he doesn't like everybody looking at him as if he's the big hero. I guess it makes some guys uncomfortable."

"Maybe." Elizabeth pushed the incident to the back of her mind. There was no sense spending the rest of the afternoon worrying about it. "I suppose it doesn't matter, now that Suzanne's all right."

Todd glanced toward the adoring throng surrounding her. "From the looks of it, I'd say so. The real question here is"—he dipped his head to kiss her lightly on the mouth—"are *you* going to be all right?"

"I don't know," Elizabeth answered, wilting against him in a mock faint. "I may need more mouth-to-mouth resuscitation."

This time Todd's lips lingered on hers. "Any better?" he murmured against her ear.

"I'll tell you when I've had enough."

He grinned. "Slave driver."

A few minutes later, as they were strolling

along the edge of the lake hand in hand, Elizabeth mused aloud, "I wonder what Jessica's doing right now." She'd been vaguely concerned about her sister ever since Suzanne had made that comment about her parents, although Jessica wasn't the kind of person who had trouble taking care of herself.

"Knowing Jessica, I'd say anything was possible."

Elizabeth groaned. "You're right about that. With Jessica, 'anything' might mean . . . well, *anything*."

Todd laughed. "The only difference is, this time you won't be dragged into it."

She knew he was thinking about all the times she'd stepped in to bail her sister out of impossible jams—and then had ended up getting burned herself. Todd disapproved of the way Elizabeth stuck up for Jessica, but by now he knew better than to say much about it. Despite Jessica's faults, Elizabeth was fiercely loyal to her twin.

Elizabeth sighed. "Well, we can be sure of one thing, at least—whatever she's getting herself into, Jessica's probably having the time of her life."

Four

Jessica felt as if she'd been hit in the chest with a sledgehammer.

Standing in the doorway was the most gorgeous male she'd ever laid eyes on.

"Hi," he said in a deep, sexy voice. "I'm Pete. Pete McCafferty."

He stuck out his hand, but she was barely aware of shaking it. She was too busy noticing the way his green eyes sparkled, the way his chestnut hair fell in sun-streaked locks over his tanned forehead. In white slacks and a blue Lacoste shirt that hugged his muscular chest, he looked as if he'd just stepped off a yacht—which he probably had, Jessica speculated.

"I'm Jessica," she said, flashing him her most winning smile.

"I know. Suzy told me you'd be visiting."

"You're a friend of Suzanne's?" she asked in surprise. He had to be at least twenty. Her mother would have an absolute fit if she went out with anyone that old! Of course Jessica *had* sneaked around with older guys a couple of times, but she'd never let her parents find out.

Pete stepped into the Devlins' apartment as if he were perfectly at home doing so, asking as an afterthought, "Mind if I come in?"

"Certainly—I mean, no, of course not," Jessica stammered, feeling unsure of herself—a rare occurrence for her. Normally she knew exactly what she was doing when it came to boys, and it usually wound up with her leading them around by the nose. But Pete seemed so much more mature and sophisticated than the boys she'd known. "If you're looking for Mr. and Mrs. Devlin, they're not home right now."

"Too bad." He cast her a sleepily seductive smile, then crossed the room, sinking into a huge, thronelike leather chair by the fireplace.

Jessica's heart picked up speed, the way it always did when she found herself teetering on the brink of some potentially delicious adventure. She'd been in New York only two days, but so far it had been such a whirlwind of strange and exotic things that she wouldn't have been a bit surprised if this handsome stranger had introduced himself by saying, "Hi, I'm Prince. Prince Charming, that is."

When she'd arrived at the airport, both the Devlins had been there to greet her. Jessica immediately liked Mr. Devlin. He reminded her of her father, even though they didn't look anything alike. Mr. Devlin was short and roundish, with thinning blond hair and a bushy mustache. But his gray-blue eyes held the same fun-loving twinkle of mischief as her father's. Mrs. Devlin was much more elegant. She was tall and gloriously thin, with the kind of cheekbones Jessica could achieve only by sucking her cheeks in as far as they would go. She wore her black hair in a skintight bun from which not a single stray strand dared to escape. When Mrs. Devlin hugged her, Jessica's only impression was of a cool draft of perfumed air.

They rode home in a hired limousine. Mrs. Devlin explained that they avoided taxicabs whenever possible. According to her, they were all "dreadful contraptions" driven by "dreadful little men." Jessica scarcely paid attention to what Mrs. Devlin was saying. She was too engrossed in staring out at the Manhattan skyline, lit up like a carnival, as they crossed the Queensborough Bridge. She was so excited she could hardly sit still.

On Saturday Mrs. Devlin was going shopping on Fifth Avenue, and took Jessica along. Jessica had brought some spending money, but she was shocked when she saw some of the prices. In Saks Fifth Avenue she picked up a pretty scarf she was thinking of buying as a souvenir for Elizabeth. When she saw the price tag, she dropped it as though her fingers had been scorched. Seventy-five dollars for that! She wouldn't even spend that much on herself!

Finally she decided that Elizabeth would just have to be satisfied with the free sample vials of perfume they were passing out in the cosmetics department—Jessica could always pretend she'd paid for them. For herself, she splurged on a pretty necklace made of twisted strands of colored beads that was on sale. It didn't compare, of course, to the fabulous gems that winked at her from under the display cases in Tiffany's and Cartier's, but she tried not to look too impressed so Mrs. Devlin wouldn't think she was hopelessly unsophisticated.

They had had lunch at the Russian Tea Room, which Jessica had read about in *People* magazine. Mrs. Devlin spent the whole time smoking skinny brown cigarettes. She hardly even touched her food, Jessica noticed. No wonder she was so slim!

Jessica was hoping for a glimpse of someone

famous—according to *People*, a lot of celebrities lunched there—but the closest she got was a waiter who vaguely resembled Paul Newman. Still, she wasn't too disappointed. Obviously the people who ate there were simply oozing with money.

And now, enthroned before her was the dream boy of a lifetime. Jessica didn't care if he was Suzanne's boyfriend or not. Why should she be loyal to a girl she'd never even met? Besides, what Suzanne didn't know wouldn't hurt her. This was definitely too good to pass up.

"Would you, uh, like something to drink?" she offered.

It suddenly crossed her mind that he might ask for something like a martini. Not that she would have minded, except that Mrs. Devlin kept the liquor cabinet locked when she wasn't around. She was sure the cleaning woman would steal from it otherwise. Jessica hoped he would want something simple like a Coke.

"No, thanks," Pete said. "I can't stay. I just came by to drop off these tickets." He produced an envelope from inside his jacket. "They're for a concert Suzy and I were supposed to go to tonight. I thought since she's out of town, Tom and Felicia might like them."

It was the first time Jessica had ever heard a boy call his girlfriend's parents by their first names. Oh, he was so unbelievably sophisticated! She felt a thrill of challenge ripple through her.

"That's too bad," she said, the corners of her mouth turning down ever so slightly. "The Devlins can't go either. They're going to some kind of party. It's a shame the tickets have to go to waste. What kind of concert did you say it was?"

"Piano. Horowitz."

"Oh, I just love him!" she trilled. The truth was, she didn't have the vaguest idea who he was.

Pete wore an amused smile. "Yes, he really is quite extraordinary, isn't he? What did you think of his latest recording of Chopin's Polonaise in A Major?"

"I, uh—" Jessica felt an unfamiliar heat climbing into her cheeks. "I thought it was very—interesting."

"You did? I found it a bit on the dry side. Too intellectual. Chopin should come from the heart, don't you think?"

"From the heart? Oh, yes, definitely."

Pete rose languidly from his chair. "Well, I really must be going."

Jessica felt a rush of panic. He was leaving, and she might never see him again. She couldn't let that happen.

"This really is a fantastic coincidence," she

purred. "Here I was planning to spend the whole evening all by my lonesome self, and you just happen to have these tickets. . . ."

Pete raised one eyebrow in a way that almost made it appear he was mocking her, but he said nothing. Jessica's words hung in the air between them. She could feel herself turning very red.

Finally she blurted, "So I was just thinking—if you still want to go to the concert, I wouldn't mind going with you."

"Fine. I'll pick you up at five-thirty," he said, as if he'd been planning it all along. "We might as well have dinner first."

Jessica would have been furious at the way he'd made her suffer—if her joy at having a date with such a fabulously exciting man hadn't been so overwhelming. Back home, her parents never would have allowed her to go out with anyone his age. Obviously Suzanne's parents were far more enlightened. Oh, just wait until Cara and Lila heard about this!

Five

It took Jessica several hours to get ready for her all-important date with Pete. She spent an hour soaking in the tub, having the time of her life trying out all the scented oils and perfumes that filled Suzanne's lavish bathroom. How could any girl be so lucky?

Next came the makeup. Normally Jessica didn't wear that much. The truth was that with her natural good looks she didn't really need it. But somehow the thought of wearing too little makeup that night seemed horribly unsophisticated.

She spent an hour experimenting with Suzanne's vast array of creams, powders, eye shadows, lipsticks, and blushes. Finally she arrived at the perfect combination. Looking at the finished masterpiece in the mirror, she couldn't resist a satisfied smile. Perfect. Pete would have to be made of stone to resist her.

But by the time she'd gone through her dresses looking for something to wear, she was ready to cry. Nothing seemed right. Everything was too casual or unsophisticated by New York standards. Her best dress—a white dotted swiss with a ruffled neckline—looked like something a choir girl would wear. She tossed it on the bed in disgust.

Then she remembered Suzanne's closet. Maybe there was something that would fit her. Minutes later she had the answer—in the form of a close-fitting black crepe cocktail dress with a plunging back. When she had tried it on and inspected the results in the mirror, she could hardly believe the transformation. *My gosh, I look at least nineteen!* She imagined Pete's reaction when he saw her, and a chill of excitement chased up her spine.

The way it turned out, though, wasn't anything like what she'd imagined.

For one thing, Pete was late—nearly half an hour. Jessica was on the verge of tears by the time he showed up. The only thing that kept her from crying was the prospect of ruining her makeup. She waited for him to offer some kind of apology, but it never came.

"Are you ready?" Pete asked, taking in her polished appearance with one quick glance.

Ready! Jessica could hardly believe her ears. Wasn't he going to tell her how absolutely stunning she looked?

She was fuming, but she took care not to let Pete know. In spite of his rudeness, he was still the most exciting guy she'd ever met. Swallowing her anger, she reached out and touched his arm. "It was so sweet of you to invite me out," she cooed, fluttering her eyelashes at him. "I just don't know *what* I would have done if I had to sit home all by myself tonight."

"Oh, I'm sure you would've come up with something," he drawled, his green eyes twinkling with suppressed amusement as he looked down at her. "You don't seem like the type of girl who ever stays lonesome for long."

Jessica giggled. "Not if I can help it."

It wasn't until he was helping her on with her coat that he finally made a comment about her appearance—only it wasn't at all what she expected.

"Isn't that Suzy's dress?" he asked.

"Uh . . . she told me I was welcome to borrow anything that was in her closet," Jessica quickly invented. "Wasn't that nice of her?"

Pete nodded. "Mmm. I thought I recognized it."

Not one word about how sensational she looked in it! How could anyone be so blind? Either that or he was purposely torturing her.

He took her to Windows on the World for dinner. It was the fanciest restaurant she'd ever eaten in—as well as the most breathtaking. It was located at the top of the World Trade Center, the tallest building in New York. Gazing out the floor-to-ceiling windows, Jessica grew dizzy with delight. Below, the glittering panorama of the city seemed to stretch on endlessly. She could even see the Statue of Liberty! Except that from this height, it looked the size of a Barbie doll.

Pete ordered wine with dinner, and Jessica was pleased to note the waiter didn't bat an eyelash when it came to filling her glass. At least one person thought she looked grown-up and sophisticated! Pete was friendly enough—they never seemed to run out of things to chat about—but he continued to keep her at arm's length. It was as if he hadn't even noticed she was a member of the opposite sex!

Pete was hard to figure out. He wasn't a bit like the boys she dated back in Sweet Valley, who were usually like lumps of wet clay in her hands. Flirting seemed to be having no effect on him whatsoever. For Jessica, that was like waving a red flag in front of a bull. She became more determined than ever to get him.

It wasn't going to be easy, though. At the concert she fought to keep from yawning. Classical music was more Elizabeth's style. Personally, Jessica preferred something with a snappy beat, something she could get up and dance to. If only Pete would hold her hand or put his arm around her. He might as well be on a date with his sister the way he was acting! Was it because he was so loyal to Suzanne? Maybe. Even so, she had to find a way of tempting him away.

"I just hate the idea of going up to that big old empty apartment all by myself," she told him as they were driving home. "I know it must sound silly, but I'm just an awful scaredy-cat. Would you mind terribly waiting around with me until the Devlins get back? Maybe we could listen to the stereo or something." She put the emphasis on the "or something."

Pete smiled. "Don't worry, Jessica. I have a feeling you won't have any trouble taking care of yourself. Sorry, but I have to run."

Jessica's hands clenched into fists in her lap, her long fingernails digging into her palms. She could feel her cheeks burning. She felt like screaming. What was the matter with him? How could he ignore her this way?

Pete's Ferrari glided to a smooth stop in front of the Devlins' Park Avenue building. He bent toward her, a smile playing at the corners of her mouth. *This is it!* she thought excitedly. *He's finally going to kiss me!* She ran the tip of her tongue over her lips and let her eyelids droop seductively. She was glad now that she'd sat through the concert. Pete's kiss would certainly be worth it. This was going to be a perfect moment.

But instead of taking hold of her, Pete merely leaned across her and flipped open the door. "Sleep tight, little Jessica," he said as she was getting out.

Jessica was left to stand fuming on the sidewalk as he spun off into the night, red taillights winking as if mocking her. Tears of anger and frustration stung her eyes.

She'd never been so humiliated in her whole life.

Six

"Has anyone seen my gold necklace?" Elizabeth asked, drifting into the kitchen. She sat down at the breakfast table. "I left it on my dresser last night, and now it's gone."

Mrs. Wakefield looked up from buttering a slice of bread she'd just plucked from the toaster. "Maybe it slipped off. Did you check the floor?"

"I even looked behind the dresser. And under the bed." She frowned. "It's as if it disappeared into thin air!"

Her mother put a plate of scrambled eggs in front of her, but Elizabeth wasn't hungry. She felt terrible about losing her necklace. The twins' parents had given them identical gold lavalieres on their sixteenth birthday. Elizabeth knew how disappointed they would be if she couldn't find it. Usually it was Jessica who was always losing things.

"After breakfast I'll help you look," Suzanne volunteered readily. Her lovely face wore a concerned look. "Sometimes a thing can be right there under your nose and you don't see it."

Elizabeth sighed. "But I really *looked*. I don't know how it could've gotten on the floor. I remember taking it off and putting it in the middle of the dresser."

Suzanne reached across the table to give Elizabeth's hand a sympathetic squeeze. "Don't worry, Liz, I'm sure it'll turn up, even if we have to spend all morning looking for it."

Elizabeth flashed her a grateful smile. "It seems so unfair. Here you are on vacation, and you've hardly relaxed a minute since you got here."

Sunday morning Suzanne had gotten up early and surprised them all with an elegant breakfast of french toast made with grated lemon peel and sprinkled with powdered sugar. On Monday she'd spent the afternoon helping Steven put a coat of varnish on an old canoe he was restoring out in the garage. The list was endless. Whenever there were dishes to be done, Suzanne was the first to volunteer. She was never too tired to run an errand, or too elegant to don a pair of rubber gloves and help with the cleaning around the house. More than once Mrs. Wakefield had teased Suzanne about wanting to adopt her.

Everyone loved Suzanne. Even Lila, who usually considered every pretty girl competition, had called one afternoon to ask Elizabeth and Suzanne over to play tennis at the Fowlers' private court. It was the first time Elizabeth could remember Lila inviting her anywhere. Afterward she couldn't believe how Lila had acted—hanging on Suzanne's every word, asking her a million questions about life in New York City.

"You know, you could really be a model," Lila had told her. "The next Brooke Shields. Just think how famous you'd be."

Suzanne wrinkled her nose at the prospect. "Maybe, but I'd probably get pretty bored just standing around having my picture taken all day long. Besides, I want to go to college. And maybe law school after that. By the time I got around to doing anything else, I'd be an old hag."

Lila seemed to find that hilarious. "Somehow, Suzy, I just can't imagine you as a hag."

"Oh, I can be a real witch sometimes." Suzanne tossed her black hair over one shoulder with a slinky movement. She smiled. "I'll have to show you my magic potions sometime."

Elizabeth laughed. "In that case, you must've cast a spell over the entire male population of Sweet Valley."

Ever since the picnic, the Wakefields' phone had been ringing almost nonstop. Elizabeth had jokingly threatened to keep score. So far Tom McKay had called twice. Aaron Dallas three times. Mr. Cool himself, Bruce Patman, had asked Suzanne out only once (Elizabeth smiled every time she imagined the look on his face when Suzanne turned him down). The front runner by a mile, however, was Winston Egbert, with twelve calls—not counting the night he serenaded Suzanne from out on the lawn.

Suzanne told them all how flattered she was but she just couldn't accept. She was only going to be in Sweet Valley such a short while, and she wanted to spend as much time as possible with the Wakefields, especially Elizabeth, who had been so wonderful to her.

This morning Elizabeth was planning on taking Suzanne to the beach. They even had a picnic lunch all packed. Todd would be picking them up in a little while.

"Never mind about the necklace, Suzy," Elizabeth said. "We can look for it later." She didn't want anything to spoil their day at the beach.

"As long as no one vacuums my room while I'm gone, I'm OK."

Mrs. Wakefield laughed. "Don't look at me. I'm not planning on doing any cleaning. I'm supposed to be going into the office today. I have to be there in"—she looked at her watch, then hastily gulped the rest of her coffee—"exactly three minutes. I have to go over those new designs with a client." Mrs. Wakefield was an interior designer.

"Don't worry about the dishes, Mrs. Wakefield," Suzanne said. "I'll take care of them." She turned her attention to Steven. "More coffee? I'm getting up anyway, so it's no trouble at all."

Steven shook his head, managing only a weak smile of thanks. Elizabeth knew he was still brooding over his broken date with Tricia. He'd been moping around the house all vacation, acting as if the world were coming to an end. Elizabeth felt selfish for worrying over a misplaced necklace while Steven was contemplating the possible loss of the girl he loved.

"Why don't you come to the beach with us, Steve?" Elizabeth urged. "You're looking kind of pale. It wouldn't hurt you to get some sun on that puny bod of yours."

"Puny? Who's calling who 'puny'?" Elizabeth was glad to see she'd managed to coax a genuine smile out of him. "If you turned sideways and stuck your tongue out, you could probably pass for a zipper."

"Don't I wish!" Elizabeth flicked her napkin at him. "So what do you say—are you coming or not?"

He shook his head regretfully. "Sorry. Can't. I've got a big exam coming up when I get back to school. If I don't hit the books, I can think of a few professors who'll be using them to hit me."

When the breakfast dishes were done, Elizabeth and Suzanne went upstairs and changed into their bathing suits and shorts. By the time they had gathered together their towels and suntan lotion, Todd was beeping his horn outside. Elizabeth took one last, unsuccessful look behind the drawers for her necklace.

"Don't worry, Liz," Suzanne reassured her, slinging her canvas beach bag over one shoulder. "I'm sure we'll find it when we get back. It's got to be around here somewhere."

"I hope you're right," Elizabeth said.

"Is it very valuable?"

"Oh, I'm sure Mom and Dad paid a lot for it, but that's not the only reason I'd hate to lose it." She touched the absent place on her neck where it usually hung. "It's just that—well, you know how it is when you get attached to something. I guess you'd call it sentimental value."

Suzanne's full mouth turned up in a sympathetic smile. "Sure, I understand. Once I lost a bracelet my father had bought me in Paris. I felt just sick about it! I couldn't stop crying for a whole day!"

She hooked an arm through Elizabeth's as they headed out the door. Still smiling, she reached into her shorts pocket with her other hand, fingering the gold necklace that lay coiled inside. *A pretty little trinket*, she thought with satisfaction.

Seven

"Oh, Todd, would you mind stopping at Mr. Collins's?" Elizabeth asked as they were heading down Calico Drive. "I have to drop off some stuff for the paper. It'll only take a second."

"At your service, madam." Todd grinned, tipping an imaginary chauffeur's cap.

Suzanne, sitting in the backseat of Todd's secondhand Datsun, giggled. "Todd, you're such a nut!"

"Better watch out," he joked. "We nuts are sensitive to cracks."

Todd turned off onto a narrow, tree-lined street, pulling up in front of a neat frame house painted a sunny yellow. A child's bike lay over-turned on the lawn.

"I didn't know Mr. Collins had children," Suzanne said, peering out the window at the bike. "Is he married?"

"Divorced," Elizabeth answered. "And he's only got one child. Teddy—he's six and a real sweetie. I baby-sit for him sometimes. Though it's hardly what I'd call work. Teddy is practically no trouble at all."

"Really? I absolutely adore children myself. If I ever get married, I'll probably have about a dozen." Suzanne reached over toward the manila envelope that Elizabeth had brought for Mr. Collins. "Look, let me run in with this. I want to thank Mr. Collins for rescuing me the other day."

Elizabeth sighed in mock exasperation. "Suzy, you're spoiling me to death! Don't you ever stop being nice?"

"Yeah," Todd agreed laughingly, "give the poor kid a break. How do you expect her to be able to put up with Jessica after all this?"

While Elizabeth pretended to strangle Todd, Suzanne hopped out of the car. No one answered when she knocked at the front door. She could hear water running, so she walked around to the back of the house. Mr. Collins was standing out on the lawn watering the shrubbery. Quietly she crept up behind him, a low, mischievous laugh escaping her. Mr. Collins whipped about in surprise, nearly dropping the hose.

"Sorry," she said, smiling. "I didn't mean to scare you."

He smiled back, but the smile didn't reach up to his blue eyes. "Don't worry, I don't scare that easily. You just surprised me, that's all. I didn't hear you come up. Is there something I can do for you?"

She stared unwaveringly into his eyes, widening her own ever so slightly. It was a game she liked to play, but half the fun of it was that most of the men she played it with didn't even know what was going on. They would start blushing and stammering, or they'd look down at their feet. It gave her such a feeling of power to control people without their even knowing they were being controlled.

Take that dopey Elizabeth, for instance. How could anyone be so naive? She'd probably spend the next hundred years crawling around on her hands and knees looking for that necklace without ever even *suspecting* that her dear, sweet friend Suzy had taken it. They were all so gullible, the whole bunch of them. None of the Wakefields knew how she was really sneering at them behind their backs. Them and just about everybody else in this little hick town.

The trouble with Mr. Collins was that he didn't seem as eager to fall into her net as the others. He stared right back without blinking or shifting his gaze. For an uneasy moment Suzanne wondered if he'd seen through her pretenses. On the other hand, maybe he just needed a little more persuasion. Teachers always put themselves up on pedestals that way. Like they were better than everyone else. Oh, how she'd like to bring this teacher to his knees!

"Liz asked me to give you this," she explained, handing the envelope to him. "But I wanted to see you anyway. I wanted to tell you how grateful I am for the way you saved my life. I never did get a chance to thank you appropriately at the picnic. I really owe you a lot."

"Forget it," Mr. Collins replied with an edge of gruffness to his voice. "I can't think of anyone who wouldn't have done the same."

He was wearing only a pair of white jogging shorts and a red bandanna to keep his longish strawberry-blond hair out of his eyes. Suzanne's gaze strayed down to his bare, muscular chest, which was deeply tanned and slick with perspiration.

"It's so hot!" she exclaimed, wilting into a nearby chaise longue. She propped her slender legs up to give him a better view. The tan she'd acquired the past few days was perfectly shown off by the skimpy yellow shorts she wore. "Mind if I steal a quick drink from the hose?"

Silently he handed it to her. Suzanne laughed merrily as the cool water bubbled over her lips and nose. She let it dribble down her chin until the front of her thin T-shirt was soaked, making it cling to her very brief bikini top. Mr. Collins couldn't help but look. Suzanne smiled to herself in triumph as she noticed the color mounting in his cheeks.

"Thanks," she said, handing the hose back to him. She looked down with a tiny cry of chagrin. "Oh, will you look at that—I'm all wet. Honestly, Mr. Collins, you must think I'm the klutziest girl in the whole world!"

He bent down to yank a weed from the grass. In a low voice he muttered something that sounded like, "I think you know exactly what you're doing." But she couldn't be sure she'd heard it right.

At that moment a blond, blue-eyed miniature version of Mr. Collins came banging out through the screen door. When he caught sight of Suzanne, he stopped and stared up at her as if he'd just discovered a movie star standing out on his back lawn.

Suzanne went over to him and put her hand

out, giving the little boy her most winning smile. "Hi, I'm Suzy. And I'll bet your name is Teddy."

His face lit up. "How'd you know?"

"I'm a good guesser."

Teddy pointed over at Mr. Collins. "He's my dad."

"I know. Aren't you lucky to have such a nice daddy?"

"Do you go to school with my dad?" Teddy asked.

"No, but I wish I did. I'll bet he's the best teacher in the whole school."

"The best in the whole world!"

Suzanne laughed. "You're absolutely right, Teddy. I'm sure he *is* the best in the world."

She straightened to face Mr. Collins. "He's adorable. I just love kids."

Mr. Collins looked fondly down on Teddy. "Yeah, he's great." For a minute Suzanne thought she'd won him over, but then he drew back. "Well, thanks for bringing this stuff by. Tell Liz I said thanks, too."

It was obviously a dismissal. Suzanne was annoyed. She'd been counting on something more—a word, a glance, some small sign that he found her irresistible. Nevertheless, she hid her disappointment behind a brilliant smile.

"Don't mention it," she replied airily. "It was the least I could do after—well, you know."

She made it sound as if his saving her at the picnic had been something private and special.

Mr. Collins blushed. As Suzanne turned to go, she wore a smug expression. The invincible Mr. Collins wasn't so invincible after all.

"Sorry I took so long." Suzanne slid into the backseat. "Mr. Collins was telling me about the paper and how great the kids who work on it are. Especially you, Liz."

Elizabeth sat up straighter. "Me?"

Todd nudged her teasingly as he started the engine. "Maybe I should be jealous."

Suzanne giggled. "He didn't mean it that way, silly. Anyway, I really think you're lucky, Liz. I've always wanted to be a writer, only I'm terrible at it."

"I can't imagine you being terrible at anything," Elizabeth protested warmly.

Suzanne grinned. *I'll just bet you can't.*

Aloud, she said, "I'm afraid I'm just not as talented as you, Liz."

"She's a hard act to follow, all right," said Todd as he turned onto the coast highway.

"Will you two stop it!" Elizabeth cried. "If you don't watch it, I'm going to have trouble squeezing my head out the door by the time we get there."

"What head?" Todd teased.

By the time they arrived at the beach, Elizabeth's side hurt from laughing so much. They all joined Enid and George by the lifeguard station, where a small village of towels, coolers, and beach chairs had sprung up. Within minutes their blanket was besieged by a crowd of boys competing for Suzanne's attention.

"How does she manage?" Enid asked Elizabeth, watching as Suzanne settled an argument between Aaron and Tom over who would rub suntan lotion on her back. "I wonder what it'd be like to have so many guys chasing after you at once."

Elizabeth laughed. "Noisy. Between the phone ringing and Winston serenading Suzy from the lawn, I'm about ready to go deaf."

"Well, at least now you know what it'd be like living with a movie star."

"You know what someone did the night before last?"

"I hate to guess."

"In the morning we found 'I love you, Suzy' spelled out on the lawn in toilet paper! Have you ever heard of anything so outrageous?"

"I wonder who did it?"

"I'll give you three guesses."

Enid grinned. "I think I only need one. Winston, right?"

"Who else would do something so nutty?"

They both giggled.

"Boy, old Win must have it bad," Enid said. "I think it's kind of nice, though. Ever since Mandy Farmer moved away, he seems to have lost his sense of humor—if that's possible for Win. It's about time he got over her. But still, this thing for Suzy looks even more drastic than his old crush on Jessica."

"Don't let Jessica hear you say that. She thinks the only reason boys were invented is so they can fall in love with her."

"In that case, it's a good thing Suzy won't be around when she gets back!"

"You're right. Jessica would be furious. But it's not as though it's Suzy's fault. She just seems to have this strange affect on men."

"That's OK," Enid said, "as long as she keeps her charm rays away from Todd and George."

"Do I hear somebody paging me?" George rolled over onto his back and propped his head on Enid's knee.

Enid tousled his sandy hair affectionately. "You can go back to sleep. I was just telling Liz how you turned down a date with Bo Derek so you could take me to the movies last night."

George winked. "Yeah, she was really persistent, too. She kept crying and telling me she was going to throw herself off a bridge if I

65

didn't go out with her. I was almost afraid I'd have to give in."

"What finally convinced her to forget it?" asked Elizabeth, biting down on her lip to keep from laughing.

With a perfectly straight face, George said, "I told her she'd never be good enough for me."

"Ugh!" Enid socked him lightly on the chest. "You're so conceited!"

"I know. It's one of the many reasons you love me, right?"

"Right." Enid leaned over and kissed his forehead.

George looked up at her tenderly. "Mmm. Got any more of those?"

"That's for me to know and you to find out."

"I can hardly wait."

"I'll bet!"

"Will you guys quit horsing around?" Todd growled in jest. "I'm trying to do some serious sunbathing here."

They all converged on him at once. George grabbed him by the ankles, while Elizabeth and Enid each took an arm. By the time Todd realized what was happening, it was too late to escape. They carried him, squirming and yelling, down to the ocean, plunging him into the surf with a single mighty heave.

Afterward Todd chased Elizabeth down the

beach, pretending to lasso her with a long piece of seaweed, until they both fell laughing into the ocean. He kissed her as a wave crashed over them. Elizabeth decided this was better than having "I Love You" spelled out in toilet paper on her lawn any day.

By the time they returned home later that afternoon, sunburned and happy, Elizabeth had pushed all thoughts of the lost necklace to the back of her mind. It was Suzanne who reminded her.

"Why don't we look for your necklace now, Liz?" she suggested as they were going upstairs. "I'll feel so much better when you've found it. I know how awful it is to lose something you really care about."

Eight

The phone rang just as Elizabeth was getting ready for bed. She was expecting a call from Todd, and so she quickly grabbed the extension in her room.

"Hi!" a voice chirped over the crackle of long-distance static.

"Jess!" Elizabeth cried. "How come you're calling? Isn't it expensive?"

"Don't worry, the Devlins can afford it," she said. "Anyway, I wanted to see how you were getting along without me."

"Fantastic!" Elizabeth blurted out. Then, realizing Jessica's feelings might be hurt, she quickly backtracked. "What I mean is, we really miss you and all, but you wouldn't believe Suzanne—she's really fantastic. I wish you could meet her."

"Yeah, I wish I could, too," Jessica said.

"Are you OK?" Elizabeth wanted to know. "You don't sound too happy."

"I don't?" Jessica said quickly. "It must be this awful connection. Honestly, Liz, I've never been so deliriously happy in my entire life. The Devlins—well, it would take me a hundred and thirty-seven years to describe *them*. Everyone around here is so fabulously rich, it's enough to make you sick!"

"I'm glad you're having such a good time," Elizabeth said. She didn't feel a drop of envy. She was having too good a time herself to care.

"I'm having a *fantastic* time!" Jessica emphasized. "Last night some of Suzanne's friends gave a party in my honor. You should have been there, Liz. They're all so *sophisticated*. There's this one girl, Evelyn—she's our age, and she's dating a guy who's *twenty-five*. She says she never gets asked for her I.D. when they go places."

"It sounds a little strange to me."

"That's because you're so inexperienced," Jessica said in a lofty tone.

Elizabeth laughed. "What's that supposed to

mean—that *you're* so experienced? Come on, Jess, neither of us is exactly Liz Taylor."

"Speak for yourself!"

"OK, what's all this leading up to?" Elizabeth asked impatiently. "I know you, Jess, you didn't call up for no reason. What gives? Or should I say *who*? Knowing you, it's got to be a boy."

"How did you guess?"

"Easy. Your track record speaks for itself. Who is he?"

"Oh, just a friend of the Devlins," Jessica hedged. "Oh, Liz, I wish you could meet him. He's the sexiest guy you could possibly imagine."

"*I* couldn't possibly imagine anyone sexier than Todd," Elizabeth declared staunchly.

"OK, then, he's just as sexy as Todd."

"Mmmm. Sounds intriguing. Tell me more."

"He's tall, dark, and handsome, with the most incredible green eyes you've ever seen—"

"I prefer brown myself."

"—and you wouldn't *believe* how sophisticated he is!"

"I'll take fun-loving over sophisticated any day."

"Naturally, he's crazy about me."

Elizabeth smiled. "Naturally."

"When we're together, he can't keep his hands off me."

70

"Uh-oh, sounds pretty dangerous."

"Don't worry, I can handle it."

"Are you sure? Remember what happened with Scott Daniels."

Scott was a college guy Jessica had thought so terrific—until he pushed her past her limits. They fought, and she ended up spending a night stranded in a mountain cabin.

Jessica groaned. "Do you always have to remind me about him? That was ages ago. Besides, this time it's completely different."

"I hope so, for both our sakes."

Elizabeth couldn't forget the way she'd been dragged into the Scott Daniels fiasco. After staying out all night, Jessica ended up missing an important test in school the next day—a test she talked Elizabeth into taking for her. Elizabeth had felt horribly guilty afterward, and her fight with Todd over the incident hadn't helped.

"Oh, Liz!" Jessica brought her back to the present. "Don't be such a worrywart. Everything's going to be absolutely perfect. It's like a dream come true. But, listen, I have to go now. I'll fill you in on all the details when I get home. 'Bye!"

As she hung up, Jessica couldn't help feeling a twinge of guilt about the way she'd lied to Elizabeth. The truth was, everything *wasn't* absolutely perfect. After the cool treatment she'd gotten from Pete, she was certain she'd never see him again. Besides all that, she was starting to feel a little homesick. In fact, she'd called Elizabeth just to hear her voice. Jessica was lonely. She felt hopelessly uncomfortable around Mrs. Devlin, who did nothing to put her at ease. And Mr. Devlin, though friendly, was always off at some embassy function or other. On all but two of the nights since her arrival, Jessica had gone to sleep before he'd gotten home. She was starting to have second thoughts about this whole trip. It was something she would never have admitted to anyone in a million years. She had even tried denying it to herself. The night of Evelyn's dinner party, for instance, she'd *thought* she was having fun at first—until things got out of hand and she realized she was in over her head.

Evelyn was Suzanne's best friend. Her family lived in a building on Sutton Place, one of the most exclusive streets in Manhattan. A doorman with gold-braided epaulets had ushered her in. At the door to Evelyn's apartment a woman in a uniform met her to take her coat and show her into the living room.

Suzanne's friends were all drinking champagne when she arrived. A tall, sleek brunette wearing an outfit that looked like silk pajamas got up as she walked in.

"Hi," she drawled. "I'm Evelyn Meeker."

Evelyn introduced her to the others, but their names were a blur to Jessica. Several of the boys eyed her appreciatively, but the girls didn't seem too interested. As soon as they'd greeted her, they went back to what they'd been discussing before.

"Daddy says real estate makes more sense," said a nasal-voiced blonde with pinched good looks. "If I put Grandmother's inheritance into the stock market, I could lose everything."

"Diamonds," piped a petite red-haired girl. "When I come into my money, I'm putting it all into diamonds."

"With the family you come from, you might need a whole room for those rocks," said a boy standing next to her.

"Oh, Simon," the redhead retorted with annoyance. "Don't be so crass."

Someone filled a champagne glass and handed it to Jessica. These people were all so sophisticated! It seemed impossible that they were the same age as she. They all appeared so much older. Quickly, she downed her champagne. Just as quickly, her glass was refilled.

"Where are your parents?" she asked Evelyn, glancing about nervously.

Evelyn gave a tinkly little laugh. "My parents? Oh, you mean like in chaperon. Don't worry— they couldn't be bothered. Besides, they're in the Caribbean right now. They always go this time of year."

Wow! Jessica thought. If only *she* could have parties like this, without her parents hanging around.

"It must be nice having the whole place to yourself," she said.

"Oh, I hardly ever stay here when they're gone. My boyfriend has an apartment in the Village. I usually stay there."

"Your boyfriend has his own apartment?" Jessica echoed incredulously.

Evelyn laughed again. "Well, he's twenty-five, after all. Don't you just *adore* older men? Honestly, boys our age are such incredible babies."

"Unfair!" cried a boy sitting on the plush beige couch. Leering tipsily at Jessica, he added, "All I ask is that you give me a chance. I may be seventeen, but I'm old at heart."

"Malcolm's OK," Evelyn whispered. "His family owns a big estate in Connecticut, and he drives a Maserati."

The woman who had answered the door announced that dinner was served. They all retired to the dining room, where a fabulous feast had been assembled as if by magic. Evelyn produced several more bottles of wine she'd "borrowed" from her father's cellar.

By the time dinner was over, Jessica was so dizzy she could hardly stand up. The room seemed to be spinning. She tried to concentrate on what people were saying, but none of the conversations made sense. What was even worse was that every time *she* tried to say something, it came out sounding garbled and foolish. On top of everything else, she was starting to feel slightly sick.

She got up in search of the bathroom, nearly tripping over a bronze urn set on the floor near the fireplace. "Ooops!" she said as she bumped into an end table, knocking over a small vase of dried flowers.

"Obviously she can't hold her liquor," she could hear someone saying through the buzzing in her head.

"What did you expect?" someone else said. "She *is* from some little town in California, after all."

Jessica's cheeks were flaming as she ducked into the bathroom. She was so embarrassed she wanted to die. Instead, what she did was simply pass out. One minute she was holding on to the sink while the floor rocked wildly beneath her. The next thing she knew, she was lying sprawled in the backseat of a cab speeding back toward the Devlins' apartment.

Nine

"I can't, Todd. I just can't. A promise is a promise."

Elizabeth stacked the last of the dinner plates in the dishwasher and flicked it on. Two tickets to a Lakers game and she had to be baby-sitting! Oh, well, Todd would just have to understand. Mr. Collins was counting on her, and she couldn't just back out at the last minute when it would be hard for him to find a replacement.

"I know it's kind of late and all," Todd said. "But I just found out myself. My cousin had to cancel, and so he gave me his tickets. Are you sure you couldn't get somebody to take your place?"

Elizabeth bit her lip. "I suppose I could ask Enid. . . . No, wait. She's going to the movies with George. I don't know, Todd. Practically everybody I can think of already has plans."

"*I* don't."

Todd and Elizabeth turned to find Suzanne standing there. She'd come in from the laundry room and was carrying a stack of freshly folded sheets and pillowcases.

"I couldn't help overhearing," she explained. "Liz, there's absolutely no reason for you to miss that game. I'd be happy to take over your baby-sitting job."

"But—" Liz started to protest.

"But nothing. What are friends for? Besides, I'd enjoy it. I think Teddy's adorable."

Elizabeth stared at her in disbelief. "Suzy, I can't let you. It's—it's too much! You're always doing things for us. I'm starting to feel positively guilty."

"Don't," Suzanne said. "I know this sounds hopelessly corny, but it just so happens I *like* doing things for other people. It makes me happy."

"Suzy, you're incredible! It doesn't seem possible that anyone could be so nice."

"You've just been living with Jessica too long," Todd muttered under his breath.

Elizabeth ignored his comment. She was too

happy about going to the game to let anything bother her.

"I'm sure it's OK, but let me call Mr. Collins first and let him know," she said.

A tiny frown creased Suzanne's forehead. Then she smiled. "Listen, why don't you let me do the phoning? You're going to be late if you don't start getting ready."

Elizabeth hesitated. "I don't know. I really should talk to him myself."

"Suzanne is right," Todd broke in with a glance at his watch. "We'd better hurry if we want to get there in time. Besides, I'm sure Mr. Collins won't mind. He's pretty easygoing."

"OK, I give up." Elizabeth threw her arms around Suzanne in a quick, fierce hug. "Thanks, Suzy. You're fantastic. I don't know how I'm ever going to repay you."

Suzanne laughed. "For one thing, you can stop thanking me. Just go and have a good time." *You can bet I'm going to do the same*, she thought.

Half an hour later, Todd and Elizabeth were dropping Suzanne off in front of Mr. Collins's house.

"Give Teddy a kiss for me," Elizabeth called as Suzanne was climbing out of the car.

Teddy isn't the one I plan on kissing, Suzanne thought, laughing to herself. She waved a cheerful goodbye as she bounded up the front steps. While waiting for her knock to be answered, she deftly opened the top button of her short-sleeved blouse.

It was all Suzanne could do to keep from laughing aloud at Mr. Collins's astonished look when he opened the door to find her standing there.

"Liz couldn't make it," she explained, sailing inside. "I hope you don't mind, but she asked me to take her place."

He frowned. "She should have called to let me know."

"Oh, well . . . she said she was going to, but I guess she forgot. She was in kind of a hurry."

"That doesn't sound like Liz. She's usually so responsible."

Suzanne smiled. "I guess no one's perfect." She leaned close to Mr. Collins, accidentally on purpose brushing up against him. She enjoyed watching him redden. "Anyway, you don't have to worry about a thing. I love little kids. Teddy and I will get along just fine."

Roger Collins's frown deepened as he glanced at his watch. "I don't like last-minute rearrangements, but I suppose it'll have to do. I'm having dinner with some friends; so it's too late to back out. Anyway, I should be home around twelve-thirty."

At that moment Teddy came bounding into the living room. When he caught sight of Suzanne, his face lit up at the unexpected surprise.

"Are you gonna baby-sit?" he asked. "Where's Liz?"

Suzanne flopped down on the couch. "Whoa! One question at a time. But first I have a question for you: Would you *like* me to baby-sit?"

"Yeah! That'd be neat!"

"OK, then let's seal it with a handshake." Solemnly she shook his chubby hand. "Later on, if you want to, I'll show you how to make a cat's cradle."

"Neato!"

Suzanne cast a demure look up at Mr. Collins. "See what I mean? Teddy and I will get along fine. We're friends."

Mr. Collins knelt to give Teddy a goodbye kiss. "OK, Bear, you know the rules. Bed by eight-thirty. And don't forget to brush your teeth."

He gave Suzanne the phone number where he could be reached. "Call me if you have any trouble—any trouble at all." Obviously he had trouble on the brain where Suzanne was concerned.

"Don't worry about a thing," she purred. "Everything will be just perfect."

After Mr. Collins had left, Teddy clambered up to sit beside Suzanne. "Do you know the story about Theodore the Turtle?" he asked.

"I don't know any stories," she replied in a bored voice.

She picked up a magazine and began flipping through it. Mr. Collins had a lot of magazines. Books, too. They were scattered all over the place. Didn't he have any hobbies besides reading? Well, she would soon find out.

"Liz knows a lot of stories," Teddy persisted.

"Well, I'm not Liz," she said flatly.

Teddy looked crestfallen. "Aren't you going to show me how to do the cat's cradle?"

"Later," she snapped. "I'm busy right now."

Teddy's big blue eyes shimmered with tears. "How come you're mad at me, Suzy? You said we were friends."

"Look, can't you watch TV or something? I *told* you, I'm busy."

Annoyed at his persistence, she jumped up and disappeared into the bedroom. Now that there was no one around to impress, she didn't have to waste time being nice to some stupid little kid. She'd only taken this job in the first place to get close to Mr. Collins. Let Teddy take care of himself. Hadn't *she* taken care of *herself* during all these years of being shipped off to boarding schools? Oh, they pretended it was for her own good, but she'd known they were only trying to get rid of her. She'd never told anyone how much she hated it—and them. Someday she would show them, though. Someday all the creeps who smiled and pretended to be her friends would find out how she really felt about them.

Meanwhile, here she was alone in Mr. Collins's bedroom. Her skin prickled at the deliciousness of it; her stomach felt floaty with excitement. She spent the next hour or so going through his closet and drawers. She wasn't looking for anything in particular—she just liked going through other people's private things; she could find out a lot about them that way. Some of the time it was even useful. Like that time she found that plastic bag of pot in her cousin Ruthie's jewelry box. Ruthie had cried and begged her not to tell—and Suzanne had kept her promise not to. Why should she? As long as she kept Ruthie's secret, she had the perfect slave. Poor scared Ruthie would do anything to keep her parents from finding out.

The contents of Mr. Collins's bedroom, however, proved mostly disappointing. She'd been unable to unearth even a *Playboy* magazine. The only things she'd learned were that he liked to dress casually, favoring cords and lightweight sport jackets rather than conservative suits, and that he was extremely fond of his son, judging from the number of photographs of Teddy she saw lying around. How boring. Well, maybe he wasn't so boring under the surface. She intended to find out.

She could hear the TV going in the other room. Good. The little brat had found something to do besides bug her. She decided to take a bath. Maybe Mr. Collins would come home early and find her in the tub, just like in the movies. Boy, would he be embarrassed. She giggled at the thought. Arranging her hair on top of her head, she examined herself in the mirror as if posing for a bath oil commercial. Yes. Definitely sexy.

By the time she'd finished taking a leisurely bath and had gotten dressed, it was past eleven. She found Teddy asleep in front of the TV. His face looked red and blotchy as if he'd been crying. Never mind. She'd tell Mr. Collins that Teddy had fallen asleep before she could put him to bed and that she hadn't had the heart to wake him up. He'd never know the difference.

Suzanne prowled around the house, switching off all the lights except for one low table lamp in the living room. She found a station on the radio that played soft, romantic music. For good measure she undid another button on her blouse and curled up on the couch to wait.

Mr. Collins arrived home shortly before twelve-thirty. Suzanne closed her eyes, pretending to be asleep. She could hear the leathery squeak of his shoes as he approached.

"Suzanne. Wake up," his voice urged.

She continued to play dead.

He bent closer. She could feel the warmth of his breath against her cheek. This time he shook her gently by the shoulder.

Suzanne let her eyelids flutter open in frightened surprise. She sat up with a gasp. "Oh, Mr. Collins, it's you! I didn't hear you come in. I must have fallen asleep. You nearly scared me to death. Just feel how my heart is beating!"

She grabbed his hand and pressed it to her chest. Mr. Collins flushed as he pulled away.

"It's late," he said. "I'd better take you home now. I don't want the Wakefields to worry."

"They won't be worried. They know where I am." She stretched sleepily, arching her back so that her chest strained against the few closed buttons of her blouse. "Aren't you at least going to offer me something to drink? I wouldn't mind a glass of wine."

"You're too young to drink," Mr. Collins stated flatly.

She laughed. "Oh, don't be so old-fashioned. My parents let me drink all the time. I'm not going to turn into an alcoholic or anything if that's what you're worried about."

"That's not what I'm worried about."

"Then what are you worried about?" she said silkily. With lazy, catlike grace, Suzanne rose from the couch and wound her arms about his neck. She could feel his muscles tensing as she pressed up against him. She knew the effect she was having on him, and it gave her a heady rush of power.

"Suzanne, stop it." Mr. Collins's voice was low with warning.

"I know what's bothering you," she murmured. "Why don't you relax. I'm a big girl. And I'm not the type to kiss and tell."

She parted her lips and tilted her head back, willing him to embrace her. He was so close, she could tell. His heart was beating too quickly, much too quickly. . . .

"Oh, Roger . . ."

Trembling with the effort, Mr. Collins pulled free from her. "Get your things," he said coldly. "I'll wait for you in the car."

She stared at him for a long, incredulous moment. She couldn't believe it. He was turning her down! She felt like screaming. How *dare* he reject her?

Her eyes narrowed to razor-thin slits. "You wanted to kiss me. I know you did."

Mr. Collins shook his head. His eyes looked almost black in the shadowy light. "You're playing a very foolish game, Suzanne. Believe me, I'm doing you a favor. Otherwise, you'd be very sorry later on."

But Suzanne scarcely heard what he was saying. Rage was boiling inside her, bubbling to the surface. He had some nerve to treat her this way! She felt like hitting him, scratching his eyes out. Oh, he'd pay for this. She'd make him pay.

Grabbing her purse, she pushed her way past him out the door. She'd be damned if she'd let him drive her home now! Suzanne was halfway down the front path when she whirled to face him one last time.

"*You're* the one who's going to be sorry, Roger Collins!" she hissed.

Suzanne calmed down as she walked back to the Wakefields'. The thought of getting her revenge on Mr. Collins was making her feel better, more in control. Already a plan was taking shape in her mind. She dried her tears. It might even be fun.

Smiling a little, she pulled at her blouse until it ripped. Let everyone think Mr. Collins had attacked her. It would be priceless, absolutely priceless. He'd probably even be kicked out of school.

As she neared the house, Suzanne let her smile drop. It took her a minute to muster up the tears again, but she managed. After all, she was an expert at it, wasn't she? Letting herself in the front door, she crept slowly up the darkened stairs toward Elizabeth's room.

Ten

"It's so romantic." Jessica sighed, sinking deep into the leather seat of the horse-drawn carriage as the twilit green of Central Park skimmed past. "I wish I had a picture of us. No one at my school is going to believe this."

"It's a bit touristy for my taste," Pete commented.

His arm was draped over the back of the seat. The tweedy fabric of his sleeve grazed Jessica's bare shoulder, sending ripples of icy gooseflesh down her back.

Jessica laughed. "Well, I *am* a tourist after all, so I guess that qualifies me. And you're my tour guide." She shot him a coy, sidelong glance.

"Pete, it's been such a wonderful day! How can I ever thank you?"

"Don't thank me, thank the Devlins. It was their idea."

"They asked you to call me?"

"They thought you might enjoy spending time with someone closer to your own age." He shrugged. "I happened to be free; so it really wasn't any trouble."

Jessica's heart plunged. She should have known it was too good to be true when Pete phoned to invite her out for a day of sightseeing. It was Thursday; she was leaving in three days. She hadn't thought she would see him again. Then, when he called . . .

So he was only doing it as a favor to the Devlins! Just when she was starting to think he might really like her!

This called for drastic action. Jessica felt a surge of determination. This time she was going to pull out all the stops. She'd bring King Cool to a boil, if it was the last thing she did!

She snuggled closer to Pete so that the breeze blew her hair against his cheek in a silken caress. "If this were a movie, we'd probably be kissing right now," she purred.

Pete arched his brow. "Do you always imagine yourself to be the star of a movie?"

"That depends on the leading man."

"What sort of leading man did you have in mind?"

She giggled, managing to snuggle even closer. "He'd have to be tall, dark, and handsome. With green eyes and a sexy smile. Very cool. Do you know anyone who might fit the description?"

"I can't imagine."

"He'd have to be a good kisser, of course, but that's the kind of thing you can't tell just by looking at someone." She knew she was flirting outrageously, but she didn't care. All was fair in love and war.

"No, of course not." Pete's eyes danced with amusement. "You should have fun auditioning in any case."

"Well, actually"—Jessica shifted to close any remaining gap that lay between them, bringing her head to rest cozily on his shoulder—"I *do* have someone in mind, but I'm not sure he's interested."

"Impossible!" He pretended to be shocked. "How could anyone resist you, little Jessica?"

Jessica pouted. "I'm not so little."

"So I'm beginning to see."

No you don't see! she raged inwardly. None of her strategies were working. She'd tried the subtle approach. Zero. She'd tried the friendly, interested approach. Ditto. Today, when they were on top of the Empire State Building, she'd clung to him, pretending to be deathly afraid of heights. He'd simply patted her hand and led her back to the elevator as if she'd been a child. Talk about humiliation!

It was getting dark and chilly. The ride didn't seem that much fun anymore. Actually, she was starting to feel a little sick to her stomach. Why was Pete torturing her this way?

By the time they arrived back at the Devlins' apartment, Jessica was on the verge of tears. She didn't care what she looked like anymore. She didn't even care how she acted. He was treating her as if she were invisible anyway, so what difference did it make?

Pete rode up with her in the elevator—she assumed it was because he wanted to see the Devlins. But no one was home when they got there. It figured. Jessica had spent the better part of her vacation alone in this apartment, after the disaster at Evelyn's. One exception was the dinner party Mrs. Devlin had given supposedly in Jessica's honor. The only other teenager was a dorky thirteen-year-old girl named Martha who wouldn't talk about anything but her horse and the summer she'd spent at a camp for overweight kids. The rest of the people acted as if Jessica hardly existed. Where were all the rich, exciting men who were supposed to be falling all over her? Certainly Pete wasn't one of them!

"Do you want a drink?" Pete now asked. "I'm having one."

"I don't think Mrs. Devlin—"

"Oh, Felicia won't mind. I know where she keeps the key to the liquor cabinet."

Jessica shrugged. What did it matter at this point? She didn't protest when he handed her a glass of brandy. She took a gulp, nearly choking as the fiery liquid burned its way down her throat. When Pete switched off the lights a few minutes later, she hardly noticed.

Suddenly he was beside her in the darkness. His breath was hot against her face. Then he was kissing her! He was actually kissing her! Jessica could barely believe that she wasn't dreaming. She responded eagerly at first, but it quickly became apparent that Pete had much more in mind than kissing.

What was going on? Nothing could have prepared her for the way he was acting after all the indifference he'd shown her up until now. He'd always been so cool, so controlled, so remote. Now he was acting *out* of control. His mouth was pressed against hers with an insistence that was frightening. One hand was sliding up over her knee while the other inched up past her rib cage with equal determination. Jessica began to feel panicky.

She twisted away. "No!"

He wouldn't listen. Pressing her back on the couch, his arms tightened around her while his mouth moved down over her throat. She struggled to sit up but found she couldn't move. She was firmly pinned beneath him.

"Pete!" she gasped. "Stop it this minute! I mean it!"

Pete only squeezed more tightly. "You're getting what you asked for, Jessica. Don't tell me this isn't what you wanted. You've been practically begging for it since the day I met you."

"I—I—I don't know what you're talking about!" Jessica sputtered in outrage. Though they were both fully clothed, she somehow felt as though she were being stripped bare.

"I think you know very well what I'm talking about, not-so-little Jessica."

She felt as if she were being crushed. She could hardly breathe. She wanted to scream, but she couldn't get enough air into her lungs. Pete lay on top of her, his moist lips devouring her neck.

"Help!" she managed to get out.

"Grow up," he growled. "What kind of a

game did you think this was? You're not playing in the sandbox anymore. This is the real world."

"I—I never wanted *this*. I only wanted—well . . ."

He uttered a harsh laugh as his lips sought out her mouth once more. "Little matches start big fires. Didn't your mother ever warn you about playing with matches?"

Jessica was both scared and angry. What had she done to deserve this? She was mad at Pete, mad at the Devlins for getting her into this—she was even mad at her sister. Elizabeth had been so quick to want to switch places with her. She probably knew how it was going to turn out and had only pretended to want to go in the first place in order to make it sound like fun.

Jessica shoved against Pete with all her strength, managing to wriggle out from underneath him. She rolled off the couch, banging her head against the coffee table.

She glared at Pete. "If you don't get out of here, I'm going to call the police!"

"And tell them what? That I attacked you after you invited me up to an empty apartment? That you practically begged me to kiss you, then changed your mind at the last minute?

Get off it, Jessica. Who's going to believe you?"

"You're the most awful person I've ever met!" she said, standing up and looking at him defiantly.

Pete was laughing. Jessica got the horrible feeling he'd planned it this way. Just to humiliate her.

"I know about girls like you," he went on. "You think it's a game. You like to tease, then the minute anyone takes you seriously, you act so innocent and pure. Well, Miss Innocence, do you still feel like kissing, or is the audition over?"

"I hate you," Jessica choked out. "I never want to see you again! You're the meanest person on earth!"

He didn't look like Prince Charming anymore, she thought. In the shadowy dimness, he looked evil and mean. How could she ever have thought he was handsome?

"Don't worry, I'm on my way," he assured her. "But I wouldn't dream of leaving you without the good-night kiss you deserve."

As he lunged for her, she tried to move out of his way but banged into the coffee table. There was a tremendous crash as a brandy glass shattered on the parquet floor. The sharp scent of alcohol stung her nostrils. She was wrestling with Pete when suddenly the lights came on in a blaze.

Jessica looked up at the horrified expressions on the faces of Mr. and Mrs. Devlin as they stood frozen in the doorway.

Eleven

"Suzy! What on earth happened? You look awful!"

Elizabeth, who had just gotten home and had been getting ready for bed, stared at her friend in shocked dismay. Suzanne was trembling as she sank down on Elizabeth's bed. Her blouse was torn, her hair a mess. There were smudges of mascara under her eyes, which were red and swollen from weeping.

Suzanne covered her face with her hands. "Oh, Liz, it was so awful! It was like a nightmare!"

"*What* was like a nightmare?"

"I can't tell you," came her muffled reply. "I'm too ashamed."

"Suzy, you've *got* to tell me what happened!"

"He—Mr. Collins—he tried to—" Suzanne broke off in a fresh torrent of sobs. When she finally looked up, her expression was one of utter misery and despair. "Oh, what's the use? No one's ever going to believe it!"

"*I'll* believe you," Elizabeth reassured her.

"Promise?" Tears continued to stream down Suzanne's cheeks.

"Of course I promise! Now tell me, please, what is going *on*?"

In a ragged whisper, Suzanne confessed. "Mr. Collins tried to—I mean he. . . . Oh, I can't say it."

"*Mr. Collins?*" Elizabeth cried in horror. "Oh, Suzanne, no! There's got to be some mistake. Mr. Collins would never do anything like that!"

"You see? I knew you wouldn't believe it. I could hardly believe it myself." She gave a deep, shuddery sigh. "He seemed so nice at first."

Elizabeth felt sick. There was a funny taste in her mouth, and a strange throbbing had started up in the pit of her stomach. Suzanne was right. She *didn't* want to believe it. Not about Mr. Collins, of all people. He was more than just her favorite teacher, he was also her friend.

Tears filled Elizabeth's eyes. "Tell me everything," she said grimly.

In a low, hesitant voice punctuated by occasional hiccups, Suzanne told the story. "He seemed different when he came home," she said. "Like maybe he'd been drinking. Only he wasn't acting really drunk, just, well . . . friendlier somehow. He asked me if I wanted some wine, and when I told him I was too young to drink, he said—he said I seemed pretty grown-up to him. Then the next thing I knew he was kissing me—and trying to unbutton my blouse. I was so scared. I didn't know what to do. I ended up running all the way over here."

Elizabeth was so stunned she could hardly think straight. "It just doesn't sound like Mr. Collins. I've never known him to act that way."

"You don't believe me?"

"It's not that I don't believe you. . . ." Elizabeth was confused. "It's just that—well, couldn't you have been mistaken?"

Suzanne shook her head. "No. It was no mistake. Look, he even tore my blouse when I was trying to get away."

Elizabeth thought of all the times she'd gone to Mr. Collins when she was in trouble or needed advice, all the times he'd helped her. He always knew how to lead her to the right decision without actually telling her what to do. He was almost like a big brother or a favorite uncle in so many ways. Hearing Suzanne's story was like having a nightmare. The worst kind of nightmare—the kind a person couldn't wake up from.

"We have to tell someone," she said. "My parents. They'll know what to do."

Suzanne grew panicky. She clutched Elizabeth's arm. "What if they think it's all my fault? That I led him on? That's what *he'll* say."

Elizabeth hugged Suzanne. "How could they think anything so terrible about you? You're the sweetest person in the whole world! My parents know what you're like."

Suzanne clung to Elizabeth as if she were drowning. "I'm so scared, Liz! Nothing like this has ever happened to me. If Pete knew, he'd be so upset. He'd probably kill Mr. Collins."

Tears were streaming down Elizabeth's cheeks. Her own image of Mr. Collins kept bumping up against the one Suzanne had painted of him. It was like trying to put together one jigsaw puzzle with pieces from another. Part of her still didn't want to believe it was true. How could Mr. Collins be capable of such a hideous thing? But the evidence was all there—Suzanne's hysteria, the torn blouse. . . .

As Elizabeth went down the hall to wake her parents, she could hardly stand up. Her knees felt weak and trembly. She knew that as soon as this got out, it would cost Mr. Collins his job, maybe even ruin his life. A tiny nagging voice inside her asked, *What if it isn't true?*

But how could she doubt that dear, sweet Suzanne was telling the truth?

Twelve

"I still can't believe it." Todd shook his head as he started his car. "Mr. Collins just doesn't seem the type to go around attacking innocent girls. It doesn't make sense."

"I know," Elizabeth said miserably, shifting around in the passenger seat so she was facing him. "It's exactly how I feel, too. But I guess we just have to accept it."

The last two days—since the scandal about Mr. Collins had broken over Sweet Valley like a tidal wave—seemed like the longest of Elizabeth's life. She couldn't sleep, and her stomach was one gigantic knot.

It began with her father going to see Mr.

Cooper, the principal, who quickly notified the members of the school board. After that the news spread like wildfire. Practically everybody in Sweet Valley was buzzing about what Mr. Collins had done to Suzanne. It was the scandal of the century, thought Elizabeth. Even worse than the time everyone had thought Ms. Dalton, her French teacher, was having an affair with Ken Matthews. At least then it had only been rumor. This was fact. There was going to be an inquiry, but that was just a formality. The truth was, things looked pretty grim for Mr. Collins.

The part Elizabeth hated the most was that so many people actually seemed *glad* about it. Mr. Collins had always been popular with the students, but some parents viewed his teaching methods as too liberal. Now they were happy to have a good excuse to get rid of him.

Elizabeth was among those who would be sorry to see him go. Even knowing he'd done a terrible thing, she couldn't bring herself to hate him. In fact, every time she thought about his leaving, she felt sick. She was glad Todd felt the same way. At least she wasn't the only one who was torn.

"What's Mr. Collins got to say about all this?" Todd wanted to know. "Has anyone asked him?"

"Dad talked to him the night it happened. According to him, Mr. Collins seemed pretty upset. But he said he wasn't going to go around publicly denying it because people were still going to believe what they wanted even though it wasn't true."

"Sounds like something Mr. Collins would say."

They were on their way over to Cara's to meet some of the other kids from school and pool their resources for Lila's birthday present. Elizabeth wasn't thrilled over the prospect of going to Lila's party that evening, but she supposed there was no getting out of it without appearing rude. Besides, Suzanne had agreed to go with Aaron Dallas, and the two couples were planning on spending some time together at the party. After the ordeal Suzanne had been through, Elizabeth wanted her last night in Sweet Valley to be fun.

Todd suddenly smacked the steering wheel with the heel of his hand. "What if Mr. Collins *is* telling the truth? What if Suzy imagined the whole thing?"

"I wish it were true," Elizabeth said. "But, Todd, you didn't *see* her. She was so upset she could hardly talk. I practically had to pry the story out of her. Besides, why would anyone make up an awful thing like that?"

"You're right." Todd made a left turn onto Cara's street. "It would be crazy to want to get a nice guy like Mr. Collins fired for no reason."

The group that was gathered on Cara's back patio was divided into two factions: the get-Mr. Collins-fired bunch versus the ones who were loyal to him, no matter what.

"I don't care what anyone says," spoke frizzy-haired Olivia Davidson, her blue eyes flashing with indignation. "I don't believe Mr. Collins would do something like that."

Olivia worked on the paper, too, and was devoted to the handsome young faculty adviser. She shared his liberal views and hated injustice just as much as he did.

"Well, *I* believe it," said Cara, who was passing out sodas. "I've always thought he was the lecherous type. I've caught him looking at me more than once. Besides, he gave me a D on my last English essay."

Todd and Elizabeth exchanged looks. Cara was one of the biggest gossips in school, as well as being Jessica's best friend. She was probably responsible for the rumor spreading as quickly as it had.

Perhaps recalling his own experience at being the center of rumors, Ken spoke up in Mr. Collins's defense. "Aw c'mon, Cara, you think every guy is looking at you. Anyway, if Mr. C was so hot for you, why'd he give you a D?"

Cara glared at him, but she had no real comeback. Elizabeth couldn't suppress a tiny smile. It wasn't often that Cara was struck speechless.

"I don't think someone should be hanged before all the evidence is heard," said John Pfeifer, sports editor for *The Oracle*. "I'm not saying he *didn't* do it. I'm just saying we should hear his side, too."

"I'm with John," Enid agreed. She, too, had suffered at the hands of gossips once upon a time when an ugly episode from her past was exposed by Jessica.

"Not me. The whole thing is just *too* disgusting for words," Caroline Pearce pronounced, giving her carrot-red hair à prim toss. "I mean, to think a maniac has been on the loose at Sweet Valley High all this time and no one even suspected!"

Tom McKay snickered. Obviously the idea of Mr. Collins as a maniac struck him as funny.

"I don't think it's a laughing matter," said Winston, shooting Tom a black look. Everyone turned to stare at him. Winston hardly ever stopped kidding around; so on the rare occasions when he got serious, people took notice.

"Poor Suzy! Think of how she must have felt. Wow, I wish I'd been there to protect her!"

"Yeah, Mr. Collins would've *died* laughing," Cara whispered to Caroline.

Elizabeth couldn't help feeling sorry for Winston. Except for a few short, happy months with Mandy Farmer, he was always falling in love with girls who were unattainable.

"Well, whatever happened, it must have been horrible for sure," said John Pfeifer.

Elizabeth sighed. "I wish there was some way of making it up to her. I know it sounds dumb, but I can't help feeling sort of responsible. After all, if Todd and I hadn't gone to the game that night, I would have been baby-sitting for Teddy and none of this would have happened."

Winston brightened. "I've got it! Why don't we use part of the money we collected for Lila's present to buy Suzy something really neat? You know, sort of a going-away present."

"Hey, that's not a bad idea," Ken chimed in. "Lila's so rich anyway, we don't need to get her anything very expensive."

"I love it!" Elizabeth cried. "I know exactly the thing to get her, too. We were out shopping yesterday, and she saw this blouse she really liked. It would be perfect for her."

Even those who still doubted that Mr. Collins had done anything wrong were enthusiastic about the idea. Driving home with Todd, Elizabeth felt better than she had the past two days. Maybe she could even manage to have a good time that night in spite of her depression over Mr. Collins.

On impulse, she decided she would also use the money she'd begun saving toward replacing her lost lavaliere on a pretty scarf she'd seen that would go with the blouse for Suzanne. After all, look at the time Suzanne had spent helping her search for her necklace! It was the very least she could do, Elizabeth thought.

Thirteen

"How do I look?" Suzanne asked as she stood before the full-length mirror in Elizabeth's room.

"Too gorgeous for words," Elizabeth pronounced. "You'd better watch out, Suzy. You may start a riot in that dress."

Suzanne smiled. "Pete gave me this dress last Christmas. Wasn't that sweet? It's a Halston—it must have cost a fortune. I'm always telling him he shouldn't spend so much on me."

"Well, in my opinion it's worth every penny. On you, at least." Elizabeth wasn't so sure how she would look in something as elegant as the off-the-shoulder white satiny dress Suzanne was wearing. She'd probably look like a high school junior masquerading as Princess Diana. On Suzanne it was naturally chic.

Suzanne laughed, bending down to adjust the straps on her cream-colored high-heeled sandals. "Oh, Liz, you could probably make a hippo feel like Christie Brinkley."

It was good to see Suzanne in such a happy mood, Elizabeth thought. Ever since the night at Mr. Collins's, she had seemed so withdrawn. Now her eyes sparkled, and the paleness was gone from her cheeks. Dressing up for the party had done wonders for her.

As for herself, Elizabeth had chosen a slightly simpler outfit for the occasion. Looking in the mirror, though, she decided she didn't look too bad. She was wearing her favorite velvet skirt and a high-necked, lace Victorian blouse. Suzanne had helped her fix her hair in a fancy french braid, into which she'd tucked a sprig of fragrant honeysuckle.

"You look as if you belong on one of those old-fashioned Valentine's Day cards," Suzanne commented. "Todd's going to flip when he sees you."

"Thanks, Suzy. I just hope Dad doesn't insist on taking our picture out by the pool the way he did the last time we got all dressed up.

Actually, it was sort of funny. Jessica was so busy hamming it up for the camera, she didn't watch where she was going and ended up falling into the water. It was her own fault, but boy, was she mad!"

Suzanne sighed. "It must be fun having a sister."

"You wouldn't say that if you knew Jessica. I mean, I love her dearly, but she can be a real pain in the neck sometimes."

Suzanne cast Elizabeth a shy look. "I know this is going to sound incredibly corny, but these past couple of weeks you've been so fantastic about everything, Liz—well, I can't help thinking of you as sort of a sister. I hope you don't mind."

"How could I mind?" Tears of emotion filled Elizabeth's eyes.

What a fool, thought Suzanne. Elizabeth was almost *too* easy to trick. The same with her whole family. Look at how they'd swallowed that story about Mr. Collins. All she had had to do was mess her hair up, rip her blouse a little, add a few tears—and presto. Oh, it was too juicy for words! It was all she could do to keep from laughing in their faces.

As far as Roger Collins went, well, he was only getting what he deserved. It would serve him right to get fired after the way he'd treated her.

I showed him, she gloated to herself. *No one can ignore Suzanne Devlin and get away with it!*

"You know, Suzy," Elizabeth continued, "I'm going to miss you like crazy when you leave."

"You're the sweetest girl in the whole world!" Suzanne gushed.

"The *second* sweetest," Elizabeth amended laughingly.

The doorbell chimed downstairs.

"That's got to be Aaron," Elizabeth said with a glance at her clock. It was exactly eight. "Todd is always at least fifteen minutes late. Lateness is like a religion with him."

Suzanne inspected her reflection one last time. Then she dabbed on some perfume and grabbed the lacy shawl that she'd dropped on Elizabeth's bed. As she was dashing out of the room, she stopped to give Elizabeth a peck on the cheek.

"Thanks, Liz."

"For what?"

"For being my friend. For helping me make sure that creep Mr. Collins got what he deserved."

Suzanne frowned, and for an instant she no longer seemed beautiful to Elizabeth. Her lovely eyes narrowed into mean slits. Hatred twisted her mouth into an ugly grimace. Then the moment passed, and Suzanne looked her old

113

sweet, smiling self again. Elizabeth blinked. She must have imagined it. Suzanne could never be ugly.

As soon as Suzanne had left, Elizabeth fished the gift-wrapped box out from the back of her closet, where she'd placed it after she'd gotten home from shopping in the afternoon. Suzanne's suitcase lay partially open on Jessica's bed. On the spur of the moment, Elizabeth decided to put the present inside it. That way Suzanne would find it the next morning when she finished packing. She smiled to herself, imagining how surprised Suzanne would be.

She was rearranging some things inside the suitcase to make more room when something glinted up at her from the folds of a skirt. Elizabeth fished it out. Her lavaliere! What was it doing in Suzanne's suitcase?

Her stomach did a slow cartwheel of disbelief. There was no possible way her necklace could have gotten into this suitcase unless Suzanne had put it there.

But why? Why would Suzanne want to take her necklace? It didn't make any sense at all.

There had to be some other explanation, thought Elizabeth. A perfectly normal explanation. She would ask Suzanne about it when she got to the party. But right then she couldn't imagine what it might be. What if Suzanne really *had* meant to steal the necklace? What if . . .

She heard Todd's car in the driveway. With trembling fingers, she hastily fastened the lavaliere about her neck and hurried down to meet him.

Fourteen

"You seem so quiet," Todd remarked, reaching out and squeezing Elizabeth's hand. "Is anything wrong?"

"I'm not sure," she answered thoughtfully. "Remember I told you I'd lost my lavaliere?"

"Yeah, I remember. You were really upset about it."

"Well, I found it."

"That's great! Where was it?"

"In Suzy's suitcase."

Todd looked confused. "How did it get there?"

"That's the part I'm not sure about. Todd, how *else* could it have gotten in there unless she *put* it there?" She shook her head. "But it's

116

absolutely crazy. Why would she do a thing like that unless she meant to—" She couldn't finish the sentence.

"Steal it?" Todd supplied. He frowned. "You're right. It's crazy. I can't imagine Suzy doing anything like that. But that's how we felt about Mr. Collins, remember?"

"How could I forget? Oh, Todd, I'm so mixed up! And I'm starting to get the funniest feeling. . . ."

"Yeah, me too. Gives me goose bumps."

Absentmindedly Elizabeth fingered her lavaliere. "Suppose, just suppose Suzy did take my necklace. Would that mean she lied about Mr. Collins too?"

"I thought you said there was no way she could have lied."

"I thought so, but—well, now I'm not so sure." Elizabeth buried her face in her hands. "Oh, no, what am I saying? That Suzy ripped her own blouse to make us think Mr. Collins attacked her? Why would anyone do such a hideous thing?"

"Maybe," Todd said slowly, "we've been looking too hard for a reason. What if there was no reason? Remember that book we all had to read in tenth-grade English—*East of Eden*? There was that beautiful girl, Cathy, who everyone thought was so sweet and wonderful."

Elizabeth shivered as if caught in a sudden draft. She remembered the book well. It was one of her favorites.

"And underneath Cathy was really rotten to the core," she finished for Todd. She wrapped her arms around herself in an attempt to stop her shivering. "But that was just a book. If someone was really like that, you'd know, wouldn't you?"

"Maybe not. Some people can be pretty good fakers. What about the time before Bill Chase and DeeDee Gordon got together, when your sister pretended to be you so that Bill would fall in love with her? And she was so convincing that Bill actually bought her act?"

Elizabeth bit her lip. "But that was just Jessica. She's never done anything *really* bad."

"No comment," said Todd, staring straight ahead as he angled the car up the steep road leading to the country club, where Lila's party was being held.

Elizabeth knew how Todd felt about Jessica— and he certainly had enough reason to feel that way, she supposed. But Jessica's past wrongs had nothing to do with the problem at hand. And anyway, if what Elizabeth was thinking were true, then Jessica would look like a Goody-Two-Shoes in comparison to Suzanne.

On the other hand, Suzanne could be completely innocent. Elizabeth was aware of the fact that her writer's imagination did tend to get out of hand on occasion. Like the night she thought their house was being burglarized, and it was only Jessica trying to sneak in through the window after curfew. Elizabeth could still remember how furious her sister had been when the police arrived.

How would she feel accusing Suzanne of stealing—and worse—if it weren't true? Elizabeth wondered miserably. Awful, that's how. Suzanne had been so nice. The possibility that she'd been faking it was almost unimaginable.

Elizabeth groaned. This was turning into more and more of a nightmare. And the harder she tried to untangle it, the worse it got. If only she could talk to someone besides Todd about it. But her parents had gone out and wouldn't be home until much later. Steven had gone over to Tricia's to try and talk to her about his own tangled-up situation. In the past, she had always gone to Mr. Collins, but . . .

"Todd," she said, "would you mind taking a short detour?"

"Where to?"

"Mr. Collins's house. I think it's about time we heard his side of the story firsthand."

Todd grinned. "I thought you'd never ask."

*   *   *

The man who opened the door in response to Elizabeth's knock was a pale shadow of the Roger Collins she knew. A stubble of beard darkened his jaw. He looked as if he hadn't slept in days. Elizabeth felt a sharp stab of sympathy, held in check by the memory of Suzanne's tearstained face.

"Uh—is it OK if we come in?" she asked hesitantly. "I really need to talk to you."

"Of course you can come in, Liz . . . Todd." At least he *sounded* like the same old Mr. Collins.

Elizabeth sat down stiffly on the edge of a chair. Todd and Mr. Collins remained standing. They were both waiting for her to say something, but she felt as if a chunk of concrete were blocking her throat.

"H-how are you?" she finally stammered. The answer to that question was obvious, but she couldn't quite get herself to say anything else.

Mr. Collins shrugged noncommitally. "I've had better days."

"You're not sick, are you?" Elizabeth asked. "You don't look very good."

"I'm sick about what happened, if that's what you mean," he said wearily.

Was he admitting that he was guilty? she wondered. Then she remembered the necklace.

If Suzanne had lied about that, she could lie about anything. Elizabeth felt hopelessly confused. She looked at Mr. Collins's blue eyes, and he met her gaze. She read sadness in his expression, and fatigue and hurt. "Mr. Collins," she finally blurted out, "is what Suzy said you did true?"

Her face was flaming with embarrassment. If a trapdoor had appeared magically at her feet at that moment, she would gladly have dropped through it.

"What do you think?" Mr. Collins asked quietly, his eyes still steady as they held hers.

Suddenly Elizabeth knew what the truth was. She knew in her heart that Mr. Collins hadn't tried to seduce Suzanne. How could she ever have thought so in the first place? Tears spilled down her cheeks, and she shook her head in answer to her own question.

"I guess I never really believed it. Not deep down. I just couldn't see why Suzanne would lie about a thing like that. I thought she was my friend. I should have known better."

"Suzanne is a very mixed-up young lady," Mr. Collins said. "I think maybe in her own twisted way she did want to be your friend."

Elizabeth shook her head in denial. "No friend of mine would have lied to me the way she did. And stolen from me. Not to mention what she's been doing to you! And to think I was actually sympathetic toward her! Oh, Mr. Collins, I'm so sorry about everything. Can you ever forgive me?"

"There's nothing to forgive, Liz. I'm not angry with you. If you want to know the truth, I'm not even angry with Suzanne anymore. Oh, I was plenty mad at first. But now I mostly feel sorry for her. She must have wanted attention very badly to do what she did."

Elizabeth rose abruptly. "Well, *I* don't feel one bit sorry for her! I feel like I've been stabbed in the back. How could I have been so blind?"

She could see it all so clearly now. She remembered the time Suzanne had almost drowned, or pretended to, forcing Mr. Collins to save her. Probably what she had really wanted was to be close to him, to make him notice her. The reason she was angry enough at Mr. Collins to make him lose his job was that he *hadn't* noticed her.

"You weren't being blind, Elizabeth, just trusting," Mr. Collins said. "There's a big difference. Don't stop trusting people, even if they do disappoint you once in a while. Believe me, Liz, in the end you won't be the loser."

Elizabeth went up to him and kissed his stubbled cheek. "Thanks for being so understanding," she said. "But you can be sure of one thing. Suzanne won't get away with this. I'll make certain of that."

"What are you going to do?" Todd asked.

Elizabeth sighed. "I don't know. But I'll think of something."

Fifteen

"Forget it, Egbert," Aaron Dallas growled. "You've already cut in twice. At least let us finish this one dance in peace."

Suzanne giggled as a defeated Winston slunk off toward the row of chairs that had been pushed back against the wall to make room for dancing. Against the other wall was a white-clothed buffet table spread with plates of tiny sandwiches and hors d'oeuvres. In the middle stood a huge cake with "Happy Birthday, Lila!" written on it. Pink and white streamers fluttered from the ceiling amid balloons that had Lila's name on them. Obviously the wealthy Mr. Fowler had spared no expense for his daughter's birthday celebration.

"Poor Winston," Suzanne murmured in Aaron's ear. "I think you hurt his feelings."

The truth was she was glad to be rid of him. The big goon had been following her around all evening. She could hardly turn around without tripping over him.

"Oh, Win can take it. Besides, I don't want to share you with him. I could get used to the idea of just you and me."

"You keep forgetting. I'm leaving tomorrow."

Aaron affected a stricken look that was half genuine. "Life around here won't be the same when you're gone, Suzy. You're going to leave a lot of broken hearts behind."

Suzanne's giggles erupted into bubbly laughter. "You'd make a wonderful actor, Aaron."

"Yeah, I've always thought so. If I don't get to play pro soccer, maybe I'll try out for *Superman Fourteen* in about ten years."

"Oh, you'd be just *perfect* as Superman," Suzanne purred, giving his muscular biceps an admiring squeeze. "Better than Christopher Reeve any day."

She gloated inwardly at the glazed look that came over Aaron's face. *One snap of my fingers and I could make you fall in love with me*, she thought. It wasn't an unpleasant thought. She was enjoying all this attention. It almost made up for the way Mr. Collins had treated her.

Almost, but not quite. The only thing that would make 'her totally happy was to stick around long enough to see Roger Collins get kicked out of Sweet Valley High.

Spotting Elizabeth and Todd as they breezed in through the door, Suzanne waved. Todd looked especially handsome in a blue pin-striped sport jacket. Too bad she was leaving the next day, she thought. It might have been fun to see what she could do with Todd. He was obviously devoted to Elizabeth, but she was accustomed to such challenges. Yes, Todd would be fun. Maybe next year she could switch places with Elizabeth instead of Jessica.

Elizabeth was walking toward her, and Suzanne noticed she wasn't smiling. Then she noticed something else—Elizabeth was wearing the necklace! *So the nosy little sneak went through my suitcase.* She was annoyed, but not terribly worried. She'd think of some excuse to pacify her. Elizabeth was so naive she'd believe almost anything.

"Suzanne, I'd like to talk to you." Elizabeth cast a meaningful glance at Aaron. "In private."

"Of course, Liz. Excuse me, Aaron." Suzanne winked at her date as she linked elbows with Elizabeth. She felt Elizabeth stiffen, but she didn't relax her hold. "You know how it is. Girl talk. I'll be right back before you know it."

Elizabeth steered her into the coatroom, which was empty. She shook off Suzanne's arm and stood facing her. "I found my necklace, Suzanne. In your suitcase."

Suzanne widened her eyes in an expression of surprised innocence. "I wonder how it could've gotten in there. Oh, Liz, you—you don't think I took it, do you?"

"How else did it get there?"

"I can't imagine, unless. . . . Let me see, I was wearing my blue sweater that day you lost it, wasn't I? Yes, I'm sure I was. It must have gotten caught on my sleeve or something. I just didn't notice it when I put my sweater back in my suitcase."

"Couldn't you come up with something better than that?" Elizabeth asked coldly.

Suzanne winced as if she'd been struck. She concentrated on making herself cry. A single tear rolled from her eye to trickle down her cheek.

"I can't believe you're acting this way, Liz! I thought we were friends."

"So did I," Elizabeth said. "But I don't think you know the first thing about friendship. Mr. Collins was right. You're the biggest loser of all."

Suzanne's eyes narrowed murderously. The mention of that name instantly made her forget all her pretenses. "Mr. Collins! What did that lecherous creep tell you? That I was the one who tried to seduce him?" She uttered a dry laugh. "OK, so what if it's true? *He* wanted it as much as I did. He would've done something about it, too, if he weren't such a saint."

"Thanks for telling the truth at last," Elizabeth replied frostily. "Now I'm going to make sure everyone else knows it."

Elizabeth started to walk away, but Suzanne grabbed her by the shoulder. Her long fingernails dug into Elizabeth's skin.

"OK, so now you know," Suzanne hissed. "But who's going to believe you? It's your word against mine. You're the one who's going to look like the liar when I get finished, Miss Good-as-Gold Elizabeth Wakefield!"

Elizabeth wrenched free. "You can deny it all you want. That's not going to stop me. I'm not going to let you get away with ruining Mr. Collins."

Suzanne gave a harsh laugh. "Go ahead then. Try to save your precious Mr. Collins if you think you're so smart. But let me warn you about something first: By the time I get through with you, what happened to Mr. Collins will seem like nothing in comparison!"

Elizabeth turned pale, but she didn't back down. Slowly she turned around and walked away. Suzanne watched her like a cat, contemplating her strategy before she pounced. This was one battle she didn't intend to lose.

She thought back on the past two weeks with Elizabeth until she remembered something Elizabeth had told her in confidence. A plan formed in her mind. She'd need a little help, though. Suddenly she spotted Cara walking toward her, heading for the restroom. Suzanne smiled. Yes, Cara would be perfect.

"I'm worried about Liz," Suzanne confided to Cara after she'd cornered her in the bathroom. "Have you noticed anything different about her?"

"Different?" Cara echoed.

"What I mean is, have you noticed her acting sort of strange for the past couple of days?"

"I'm not sure I know what you mean."

"Well . . . Liz told me about the time she was recovering from that motorcycle accident she was in. Do you remember how she was acting then?"

"Do I ever! She was even wilder than Jessica. I guess you don't know how Jessica can be, but—well, it was like Liz had turned into someone else." She clapped a hand over her open mouth. "Oh, God, do you think it could be happening all over again?"

"I don't know if this has anything to do with it, but yesterday she hit her head against the side of the pool when we were swimming. She really cracked it hard, too. And ever since then . . ." Suzanne bit her lip in mock consternation. "You promise you won't spread this around? I wouldn't want Liz to be hurt. I love her just like a sister."

"You can trust me," Cara promised. "I won't tell a soul."

"It's so strange. All of a sudden she doesn't seem like the person I've gotten so friendly with this vacation. She's—"

"Go on," urged Cara, her eyes wide as Frisbees by now.

"Well, she's been *really* weird about this Mr. Collins business. Ever since she hit her head, she's been acting suspicious of me—as if she thinks *I'm* the one who went after Mr. Collins instead of the other way around."

"It sounds so crazy. Poor Liz! What are you going to do about it?"

"Please don't tell anyone," Suzanne pleaded. "I think it would be best if I talked to her parents first. It's just that I had to tell somebody or I'd burst. And I had a feeling I could trust you, Cara."

"Oh, don't worry, my lips are sealed," Cara assured her.

"Thanks, I knew I could count on you. The

main thing is finding a way to help Liz."
Suzanne sighed. "I just hope it isn't too late."

This was too much for Cara. It was all too apparent from her wide-eyed expression that Suzanne's insinuations had conjured up images of men in white coats carrying Elizabeth off in a straitjacket. Suzanne bit the inside of her cheek to keep from laughing out loud.

As the two girls were walking back to the party, Cara spotted a familiar face. "Uh, excuse me," she said. "I wanted to go wish Lila a happy birthday."

Moments later Cara and Lila were huddled together by the refreshment table, whispering furiously to each other. A feeling of triumph swelled inside Suzanne. Another fifteen minutes, she thought, and everyone there would think that Elizabeth was going off the deep end.

Sixteen

Caroline Pearce grabbed Enid as she was making her way toward the refreshment table.

"What's going on with Elizabeth?" she asked conspiratorially. "Lila just told me she heard that something's wrong with her. Is it true?"

Enid stared blankly at Caroline. "I don't know what you're talking about."

Caroline sucked in her breath. "Really, Enid. I'd think you'd be more sensitive to your best friend's problems."

"Problems? What problems? Who has Lila been talking to?"

"How should I know? But everyone's noticed how strange Liz has been acting—kind of like she was after the time she had that motorcycle accident."

"That was ages ago," Enid said quickly. "Liz is just fine now. I'm her best friend. I would know if something were wrong, wouldn't I?"

"Sometimes best friends are the last to know," Caroline said, arching an eyebrow. "I'd keep a close watch on Liz if I were you."

"And if I were *you*," Enid replied angrily, "I wouldn't go around spreading rumors that you have no way of confirming."

"Who, me?" Caroline asked innocently.

Enid was close to tears as she hurried off. There was no point in telling Caroline to keep quiet. Everyone knew she was one of the biggest gossips in school. Even if the rumor wasn't true, she'd have everyone believing it before long.

Enid had to find Elizabeth. She had to warn her before things got out of control.

Elizabeth was busy looking for Todd, who had disappeared into the crowd during her showdown with Suzanne, when Enid came rushing up to her.

"You won't believe it, Liz! Caroline Pearce is telling everyone that she heard you were having huge problems, that there's something wrong with you, that your parents are getting professional help for you." Tears filled Enid's big green eyes. "Who could have started such an awful rumor?"

Elizabeth felt a renewed surge of anger. She'd underestimated Suzanne. Even before Elizabeth had been able to spill the truth about her, Suzanne was countering with an attack of her own. Was there nothing she wouldn't stoop to?

"Come on, Enid," she said, tight-lipped. "Let's go find Suzanne. I think there's something you should know about our too-good-to-be-true friend."

Dumbfounded, Enid followed Elizabeth over to where Suzanne stood, surrounded by her usual throng of admirers. Trembling with outrage, Elizabeth marched up to her.

In a loud voice, she said, "I want you to stop telling lies about me."

Suzanne pretended complete shock. "Liz, what are you talking about? Why on earth would I want to tell lies about you?"

Cold fury mounted in Elizabeth. Unlike her twin, she didn't get angry very often, but on the rare occasions when she did lose her temper, she was known to cause even the indomitable Jessica to back down.

"I know what you're up to," Elizabeth said. "You're trying to get everyone to think there's something wrong with me so they won't believe it when I tell them what you did."

Suzanne exchanged a pitying, "see what I mean?" glance with Bruce Patman.

"I know you don't mean any of this, Liz," she said in a soft, conciliatory voice—the way one might talk to a child who's being unreasonable. "After all, you did hit your head awfully hard yesterday. Maybe you should go home and lie down."

Elizabeth frowned. "I never—"

"Oh, don't tell me you've forgotten already! Let me help you remember. We went swimming, and you cracked your head against the side of the pool doing laps."

"You're making it up. I never even went swimming yesterday!"

"Why would I want to make up a thing like that? Liz, you're absolutely my dearest friend! I would simply die if anything happened to you!"

"I'd rather have a rattlesnake for a friend!" Elizabeth cried in a choked voice. "After what you did—stealing my necklace, making up that terrible story about Mr. Collins—"

Suzanne slid an arm around Elizabeth's shoulders. "Poor Liz. You're imagining things again. How could I have stolen your necklace? You're wearing it. Look, you're probably just tired. I really think you should get some rest. Tell Todd to take you home. And don't worry about Lila—I'm sure she'll understand."

Elizabeth pushed Suzanne away. "There's nothing wrong with me! You're the one who—"

Her protests were swallowed by the buzz of the crowd that had gathered around them. Elizabeth was shaking with anger, but Suzanne's cool seemed to remain intact. It was at that moment that Elizabeth realized she was dealing with no ordinary liar. Suzanne was a monster. Her beauty was all on the surface. Underneath she was pure poison.

Elizabeth waited for some of the noise to die down. "Mr. Collins was right about you. He knew from the beginning how evil you were."

At the reminder of Roger Collins, the corner of Suzanne's mouth turned up in a tiny, almost imperceptible sneer. But Elizabeth didn't miss it. A spark of hope flared inside her. *Maybe I can crack her angelic veneer after all*, she thought.

"No wonder he wouldn't look twice at you," she added for good measure, mimicking a tone she'd heard Jessica use on numerous occasions.

At that moment Winston jostled his way through the crowd, holding a cup of punch. He extended it toward Suzanne, a foolish grin pasted across his face.

"I thought you might be getting thirsty," he gushed. Literally tripping over his own feet, he lurched forward, spilling the entire contents of the cup down the front of Suzanne's beautiful white dress. Instantly he was full of tortured contriteness. "Oh, wow, I'm really sorry, Suzy! Gee, I hope your dress isn't ruined! I don't know how I could have been so clumsy!"

Suzanne stood frozen for a long, speechless moment, as if she didn't quite believe what had happened. Then she looked down at the huge reddish stain seeping into the expensive fabric. This was clearly the last straw in an evening that wasn't turning out at all the way she'd planned. The color drained from her face. The same ugliness Elizabeth had glimpsed earlier that evening flashed to the surface once again.

"You idiot!" Suzanne shrieked. "Look what you've done!"

"Gosh, Suzy, I really feel awful about it. Here, let me help you." Winston made a clumsy attempt at mopping up the front of Suzanne's dress with a crumpled handkerchief he'd fished from his pocket.

Suzanne shoved him away. "Get off me, you dumb clod! You're only making it worse! Can't you just leave me alone? You've been following me around like some kind of big, stupid dog ever since I met you."

Suddenly she realized everyone was staring at her. Abruptly she stopped screaming. Her sweet, smiling mask shifted back into place. She even attempted a weak laugh, as if the whole thing had been a joke, as if she hadn't really meant all those cruel things she'd said to Winston. But it was too late. The suspicious looks that had been directed at Elizabeth a minute ago were now on her.

"Never mind, Winston," she simpered. "It was just a silly accident. I'm sorry I blew up at you. I was getting tired of this dress anyway, so you probably did me a favor." Turning to Aaron, she cooed, "Would you mind taking me home so I can change? I must look an absolute disaster."

Aaron gave her a calculating look and said coolly, "I don't know, Suzanne. I think it suits you just fine the way it is."

He started to walk away, and Suzanne screeched, "How dare you treat me this way! I was only doing you a favor by going out with you in the first place."

Aaron didn't look back. He just kept on walking. Suzanne cast frantically about for a replacement, but they were all walking away, some of them looking over their shoulders in disgust. All her admirers. This couldn't be happening! Not to her!

Her face crumpled, and she began to cry in shrill, noisy gasps. They were the first real tears she had shed in a long time.

* * *

"I should probably thank you, Win," Elizabeth said when she'd caught up with him at the refreshment table.

"Thank me? What for?" Winston looked up from a plate piled high with food.

"That was the best-timed accident I'd ever seen. You really saved me."

"Yeah, I know. I heard you talking to Suzanne in the coatroom."

"You knew?"

He shrugged. "Yeah. It made me realize how stupid I've been. Falling for someone without getting to know what she was really like. I should be the one thanking you, Liz. For setting me straight. As for the accident, well"—he winked—"let's just say that clumsiness comes in handy sometimes."

"Oh, Winston, you spilled that drink on purpose. I love you!" Elizabeth cried, kissing him on the cheek.

"You're lucky I'm not the jealous type," Todd growled, wrapping his arms around her from behind. "Where've you been, anyway? I've been all over the club grounds looking for you."

"I was having a private talk with Suzanne in the coatroom. And then"—Elizabeth paused to smile at Winston—"Win and I were taking care of a little unfinished business."

"So I heard. The whole place is buzzing about what happened. Sorry I missed all the action. Guess you really showed Suzanne up."

"The main thing is that now Mr. Collins won't have to lose his job. I think we have enough witnesses who'll tell the school board what that girl is really like. And Winston and I heard her admit she was lying. I don't think she'll be able to do any more damage now."

"Boy, Jessica is going to be mad when she hears about all the stuff she missed out on," Winston commented, cramming an entire chopped-olive sandwich into his mouth at once.

Elizabeth laughed. "Knowing Jessica, I'm sure she'll have a few stories of her own to tell."

Seventeen

Home, sweet boring home, Jessica thought as she, her parents, and Steven entered the house. Instantly she flung herself into Elizabeth's arms. She never thought she'd be so happy to be back in dull old Sweet Valley, but after the "excitement" of New York, she could use a little dullness. For a little while, at least. Jessica rarely went for long without a fasten-your-seatbelt thrill of some kind.

"Would you believe I actually missed your ugly face?" Jessica gushed, as Elizabeth helped her upstairs with her suitcases.

"Hey, watch who you call ugly," Elizabeth warned with a laugh. "You're talking about yourself, too, you know."

"In that case, I take it back. You're absolutely gorgeous. I was just getting back at you for not coming with Mom and Dad to meet me at the airport. Where *were* you?"

Elizabeth sighed. It was such a long story. Suzanne . . . the stolen necklace . . . Mr. Collins. Elizabeth's own head was still spinning over the whole ugly mess. She didn't want to think about it right then. And if she ever heard Suzanne's name again, it would probably be too soon. Jessica would know what had happened soon enough—probably the minute she phoned Cara.

"Uh, sorry, Jess, I just didn't feel like riding to the airport, that's all."

It wasn't a lie, really. The prospect of a chilly ride with Suzanne had been enough to quell her excitement at seeing Jessica again. Suzanne hadn't spoken a word to her since Lila's party. She hadn't even bothered to say goodbye.

Jessica acted hurt. "I suppose you and what's-her-name were having such a fabulous time you didn't even know I was gone. What was she like? Mom and Dad didn't tell me anything!"

A smile tugged at the corners of Elizabeth's mouth, but she held it in. "Oh, Suzanne was really—something else."

Jessica felt a pinprick of jealousy. Things hadn't worked out at all the way she'd imagined. *She* was the one who was supposed to have had all the fun, not Elizabeth. Instead, the tables had been turned. It wasn't fair!

After they deposited the suitcases in Jessica's room, Elizabeth pulled Jessica into her own room. "Now, I want to hear everything about your trip—and don't you dare leave out a single detail. I'm dying to know who this mystery man is." Elizabeth sat down on her bed and tugged Jessica down beside her.

"Oh, him." Jessica had forgotten all about the phone call to her sister before she'd found out what Pete was really like. "His name's Pete McCafferty."

"Suzanne's boyfriend! *He's* the mystery man?" Elizabeth broke into a huge grin.

"What's so funny?" Jessica wanted to know.

"Oh, nothing. I was just wondering what Suzanne would do if she knew, that's all. What's he like?"

"A real dream," Jessica said.

Well, it was true, wasn't it? Nightmares were dreams. Anyway, why not let everyone think she'd had a fantastic time in New York. It would be humiliating if they knew the truth.

"He sounds breathtaking," said Elizabeth.

"Oh, he's certainly that." *How could I catch my breath with him on top of me?*

"You really fell hard for him, I can see."

143

"Positively." *Like falling off the Empire State Building*.

"And he's crazy about you, too, right?"

"Insanely."

Inexplicably, Elizabeth's grin broadened. Jessica was confused. If Elizabeth and Suzanne were such good friends, why should she be happy about her sister stealing Suzanne's boyfriend? It didn't make sense. What was the big joke? Elizabeth couldn't possibly have found out the real story about Pete, could she?

Jessica's mind whirled back to that awful night when Suzanne's parents had walked in and found her struggling with Pete in their living room. The second the lights were on, Pete had snapped to his feet, red-faced and sputtering apologies right and left. Jessica had taken the more direct approach—she'd burst into tears. The Devlins immediately took pity on her and assumed the whole thing was Pete's fault— which, of course, it was. They told him they never wanted to see him again, and neither would Suzanne when she discovered the truth about him.

"Anyway," Elizabeth said, giving her sister a hug, "I *am* glad you're back. It was getting a little too boring around here without you."

Jessica brightened. "You really mean it?"

"Sure. What would we do without you to stir things up now and then?"

"I'm not sure that's a compliment, but I'll let you off this time. Hey, what's this?"

Jessica spied the gift that was still sitting on Elizabeth's dresser, the one that had been intended for Suzanne. Elizabeth had been planning to return it to the store for a refund, but she could see it was too late now. Jessica had seized it and was tearing the paper off.

"Oh, Liz, you didn't have to get me a welcome-home present—but I'm so glad you did. You're the sweetest sister in the whole world! How did you know? It's exactly the blouse I wanted. And a scarf to match!"

Elizabeth sighed in defeat. *Hang on tight. Here we go again*, she thought.

Later on, after Jessica had finished trying on the blouse and admiring her reflection from a hundred different angles, she wanted Elizabeth to give her a complete update of everything that had happened while she was gone. Especially where their brother was concerned.

"Steve hardly said a word on the way home from the airport," Jessica reported. "He acted like he was at a funeral. Honestly, you'd think he would have been a little more excited to see his own sister."

"It's got nothing to do with you," Elizabeth reassured her. "He's just upset about Tricia."

"Is she still trying to dump him?"

"Come on, Jess, she's only broken a couple of dates. I honestly don't think that qualifies as dumping someone."

Jessica sniffed. "Call it what you like, but if you ask me, I think he'd be better off without her anyhow. It's positively humiliating having my own brother dating a girl from one of the worst families in town."

"I'm glad to see you're so concerned about it from Steven's point of view," Elizabeth commented dryly.

"Well, if you cared just the teensy-weensiest bit about your own reputation, you'd be embarrassed, too!"

"I'm more worried about Steve than I am about either of our reputations. He's really been down over this thing. You should have seen his face when Tricia called this morning to cancel their latest date."

"Oh, he'll get over it," Jessica predicted blithely. "Come on, let's go talk to him. I'll bet we could cheer him up if we tried."

"Jess, I don't think—"

But Jessica had grabbed her hand and was

dragging her down the hallway to Steven's room. Elizabeth didn't even have a chance to finish her sentence.

They found Steven hunched at his desk, staring glumly out the window instead of at the textbook that lay open in front of him. Jessica flopped down on the bed.

"Hey, Steve, you want to hear a good joke? A girl sitting next to me on the plane told it to me."

He glanced at her, then went back to staring out the window. "Not now, Jess. I'm not in the mood."

"Oh, come on, it can't be *that* bad. Forget about Tricia. If she won't go out with you, I can think of plenty of other girls who would. She's not the only girl in the world, you know."

"To me she is."

Jessica rolled her eyes. "How did I ever end up with such a softhearted brother?"

"Don't pay any attention to her, Steve," Elizabeth put in. "Tricia's lucky to have someone who feels the way you do about her."

"It doesn't matter," Steven said mournfully. "How I feel about Tricia isn't the problem. It's how she feels about me. Or *doesn't* feel, I should say. I thought maybe it was my imagination, the way she was acting. But this morning, when she called off our date, I—well, I just don't know what to think anymore. I wish I knew what was wrong."

"Maybe someone else is what's wrong," Jessica suggested nastily.

Steven's expression grew stormy. "Tricia wouldn't do that! She wouldn't sneak around behind my back with another guy. I know her better than that."

"If you know her so well, how come you can't figure out why she's being so cold?" Jessica asked. "Honestly, you men can be so *naive* sometimes."

"Not every girl is like you, Jess," Elizabeth pointed out.

Jessica frowned. "And just what is *that* supposed to mean?"

"It means that just because *you* wouldn't think twice about sneaking around behind someone's back, it doesn't have to be the same with Tricia."

Jessica stood up haughtily. "Whatever you say. Of course, I should have known that Tricia could *never* do anything wrong. She probably broke your date so she could go to church."

"That isn't funny, Jess," Steven growled.

"Or maybe she's busy nursing her sick father back to health."

Steven grabbed a pillow, brandishing it threateningly in Jessica's direction. "I'm warning you. . . ."

"OK, I can take a hint." Jessica scooted out of the way, blowing her brother a kiss on her way out the door. "You know it's only because I care about you, Stevie. It would just break my heart to see my favorite brother get hurt."

"What favorite brother? I'm your *only* brother!" he called after her. When she was gone, he gave Elizabeth a look of despair. "Do you think she could be right? Do you think Tricia is seeing someone else?"

"Don't let Jessica get to you," Elizabeth advised. "She's just being her usual meddling self."

"Maybe . . ." Steven nibbled on the end of his pen. Elizabeth could feel his anguish. "Oh, Liz, it would just kill me if she was seeing some other guy!"

Poor Steven! Elizabeth wished there was some way she could comfort him, but the truth was she felt just as uncertain about Tricia's feelings as Steven did at this moment. As much as Elizabeth liked Tricia, she couldn't help wondering if there was some truth in what Jessica was suggesting. Why else would Tricia be acting so secretive?

On the other hand, her recent experience with Suzanne had taught her that appearances could be deceiving. It was best not to form judgments based on superficial evidence.

"You can't be sure of anything until you talk to Tricia," Elizabeth said gently.

Steven was close to tears. "I've tried. But—but she says nothing is wrong. Liz, I know she's hiding something. I can see it in her eyes. And it's driving me crazy!"

What terrible secret is Tricia keeping from Steven? Find out in Sweet Valley #12, WHEN LOVE DIES.

☐	25033	**DOUBLE LOVE #1**	$2.50
☐	25044	**SECRETS #2**	$2.50
☐	23972	**PLAYING WITH FIRE #3**	$2.25
☐	23730	**POWER PLAY #4**	$2.25
☐	25043	**ALL NIGHT LONG #5**	$2.50
☐	23938	**DANGEROUS LOVE #6**	$2.25
☐	24001	**DEAR SISTER #7**	$2.25
☐	24045	**HEARTBREAKER #8**	$2.25
☐	25026	**RACING HEARTS #9**	$2.50
☐	25016	**WRONG KIND OF GIRL #10**	$2.50
☐	24252	**TOO GOOD TO BE TRUE #11**	$2.25
☐	25035	**WHEN LOVE DIES #12**	$2.50
☐	24524	**KIDNAPPED #13**	$2.25

Prices and availability subject to change without notice.

Buy them at your local bookstore or use this handy coupon for ordering:

Bantam Books, Inc., Dept SVH, 414 East Golf Road, Des Plaines, Ill. 60016

Please send me the books I have checked above. I am enclosing $_____
(please add $1.25 to cover postage and handling). Send check or money order
—no cash or C.O.D.'s please.

Mr/Mrs/Miss _____

Address_____

City_____ State/Zip_____

SVH—2/85

Please allow four to six weeks for delivery. This offer expires 8/85.

You'll fall in love with all the Sweet Dream romances. Reading these stories, you'll be reminded of yourself or of someone you know. There's Jennie, the *California Girl*, who becomes an outsider when her family moves to Texas. And Cindy, the *Little Sister*, who's afraid that Christine, the oldest in the family, will steal her new boyfriend. Don't miss any of the Sweet Dreams romances.

☐	24327	SECRET IDENTITY #22 Joanna Campbell	$2.25
☐	24407	FALLING IN LOVE AGAIN #23 Barbara Conklin	$2.25
☐	24329	THE TROUBLE WITH CHARLIE #24 Jaye Ellen	$2.25
☐	22543	HER SECRET SELF #25 Rhondi Villot	$1.95
☐	24292	IT MUST BE MAGIC #26 Marian Woodruff	$2.25
☐	22681	TOO YOUNG FOR LOVE #27 Gailanne Maravel	$1.95
☐	23053	TRUSTING HEARTS #28 Jocelyn Saal	$1.95
☐	24312	NEVER LOVE A COWBOY #29 Jesse Dukore	$2.25
☐	24293	LITTLE WHITE LIES #30 Lois I. Fisher	$2.25
☐	23189	TOO CLOSE FOR COMFORT #31 Debra Spector	$1.95
☐	24837	DAY DREAMER #32 Janet Quin-Harkin	$2.25
☐	23283	DEAR AMANDA #33 Rosemary Vernon	$1.95
☐	23287	COUNTRY GIRL #34 Melinda Pollowitz	$1.95
☐	24336	FORBIDDEN LOVE #35 Marian Woodruff	$2.25
☐	24338	SUMMER DREAMS #36 Barbara Conklin	$2.25
☐	23340	PORTRAIT OF LOVE #37 Jeanette Noble	$1.95
☐	24331	RUNNING MATES #38 Jocelyn Saal	$2.25
☐	24340	FIRST LOVE #39 Debra Spector	$2.25
☐	24315	SECRETS #40 Anna Aaron	$2.25
☐	24838	THE TRUTH ABOUT ME AND BOBBY V. #41 Janetta Johns	$2.25
☐	23532	THE PERFECT MATCH #42 Marian Woodruff	$1.95
☐	23533	TENDER-LOVING-CARE #43 Anne Park	$1.95
☐	23534	LONG DISTANCE LOVE #44 Jesse Dukore	$1.95
☐	24341	DREAM PROM #45 Margaret Burman	$2.25
☐	23697	ON THIN ICE #46 Jocelyn Saal	$1.95
☐	23743	TE AMO MEANS I LOVE YOU #47 Deborah Kent	$1.95

<u>Prices and availability subject to change without notice.</u>